1066

TURNED UPSIDE DOWN

by
Joanna Courtney, Helen Hollick
Anna Belfrage, Richard Dee
G.K. Holloway, Carol McGrath
Alison Morton, Eliza Redgold, Annie Whitehead

With a foreword by C.C. Humphreys.

Includes discussion suggestions for schools and reading groups.

TAW RIVER

P R E S S

CONTENTS

READERS' COMMENTS

"1066 Turned Upside Down is the exemplar for how analytical counterfactual history should be done, combining the best elements of fiction and non-fiction to create an immensely impressive achievement."

"As a collection, the quality of the writing is exceptional and the variety of possible outcomes presented is truly fascinating."

"The collection is assembled in such a way that between the 'alternatives' are the related facts as they happened, as far as historians and archaeologists know – which still leaves room for these experienced writers' imaginations."

"A book I will read and re-read. I heartily recommend it"

"The real joy of a collection of stories like this is, of course, that you are likely to be introduced to writers you may not have come across before."

FOREWORD

C.C. HUMPHREYS

'Here lies our leader, in the dust of his greatness.
Who leaves him now, be damned for ever.'

It was the first time I cried while reading. The book: 'Hounds of the King' by that near-forgotten wizard of the craft, Henry Treece. Beornoth, the boy favoured by Harold Godwinson, arrives late and sick on that dread October day, to hear the Huscarles' death chant. Their leader, the last English King, is dying. They are going to die with him. And Beornoth, his own tears streaming, knows where he has to be and runs through the Norman ranks to join them.

I was perhaps nine when I wept thus. Yet when I look at the book now, the copy I found in some second hand store – Harold on the cover with his bandaged eye, under his Fighting Man banner, the last of his weary men turning to face the final Norman assault – I tear up again.

I have revisited that scene often. In my own writing, it is always sacrifice that gets to me – for a prince, a country, a lover. A cause. In my novel 'Possession', (part of 'The Runestone Saga'), I finally tackled the battle itself. Oh, the urge to rewrite the history! To make Harold triumph. How I longed to do it – but couldn't. For me it is still the greatest 'what if?', giving rise to lots of subsidiary ones. What if the Northern earls had smashed Hardrada at the first of the three battles that year, Fulford, sparing Harold Stamford Bridge? What if the Northerners had arrived in time for the third, at Hastings? What if Harold had rested a week? Brought more archers? Taught the fyrd not to fall for false retreats? Kept his shield raised to the sunset sky and its steel-tipped rain?

All these possibilities, and many more, are explored in the book you hold now. Because you, dear reader, have a treasure here – an ebook that imagines, in eclectic and wonderful stories, a very different 1066. These writers have taken 'the facts' (and all historical fiction writers are very chary of so-called facts!) and used them in diverse ingenious ways. I won't detract from their magnificent achievements with spoilers. But if, like me, you yearn for a better outcome to that pivotal year, you will be endlessly intrigued and satisfied here. For there are military solutions, assassinations, the intervention of God (or Gods!), the enterprise of strong women. There is an alternative history of the world where the pagan sits alongside the Christian. Where a story is rewritten – in thread! There is, of course, a time machine – for which of us historical fiction nuts, readers or writers, hasn't longed for one of them? To go back and observe – or maybe, just maybe, alter something? One little thing, so that Harold wins at Senlac and the whole world shifts.

I admit. I am biased – and more than a touch confused. I am half-Norwegian so part of me stands in Hardrada's shield wall. My surname is Norman – for Baron Homfrey came with William and was given lands in South Wales as a reward, hence the plentitude of Humphreys (and Humphries) there. But I am not a Welsh Homfrey – I am English. That's why I cry when Beornoth runs to die beside his king. That's why the hairs still rise on my arm every time the army shouts down the hill: 'Ut! Ut!' – 'Get out of my country!'

These stories deal with the 'what if?' of the year. What I hope to see next from this talented group is another collection dealing more fully with the results of that change. Would England, as Joanna Courtney wonders, have been part of an Empire of the North? Would we have expanded West, rather than being sucked into Europe's endless quarrels? Cecilia Holland once speculated that the Northerners would have moved easily, along the established Viking routes, into North America. First fighting against, then allying with, that other great warrior race (who also fascinate me) the Iroquois. What kind of world might that have been?

Alas, (perhaps!) we'll never know – but it's wonderful to try and imagine it. What you hold now is a great launch pad for further speculations. Revel here in these distinct voices; in what might have been. Then imagine for a moment, like me, that when Beornoth reaches his fallen king, that Harold is not fallen at all. It's a ruse, he is hoisting high the Fighting Man banner, signalling the counter attack that finishes the Normans and kills William the Bastard. That's a place, and a time, I'd like to be – and you can be, in the worlds and the words that follow.

C. C. Humphreys
2021

INTRODUCTION

Writers of historical fiction are, inevitably, a little bit geeky and when it comes to a year like 1066 we love nothing more than a good 'what if' conversation. Having steeped ourselves in research for our fiction, we are all more than aware of the key turning points in this momentous year and, indeed, have used them to dramatic effect in our own tales of what really happened. But what could be more fun than exploring what *nearly* happened instead?

One of the joys (and the frustrations) of the pre-1066 period is how little we truly know about it. Records are scant, most architecture is long gone, and although archaeology can still sometimes turn up a wonderful new treasure-trove of possible information, we have to accept that there are some things we will never know about the political twists and turns of the events leading up to the Battle of Hastings. But that does not stop us speculating endlessly about it.

In this respect, fiction is a gift as it lets us take all the facts we have and fill in the gaps to turn them into a credible narrative. This is the closest we can currently get to time-travel (although Richard Dee's story might have you believing differently...) but we all have slightly different opinions on the hows and whys of events and hopefully readers can appreciate and enjoy those disparities.

Within this collection, therefore, you will find some variations in terms, names, and even timelines. We do not, for example, know for sure when Harold married Edyth of Mercia, so in one story you will find that significant event in 1066, and in another in 1065. Similarly, although we know that William lost some ships while moving up the coast to St Valery sometime in late August, we do not know if this was in storms or in a suppressed sea-battle with Harold – and those ships are the subject of speculation in more than one of these stories.

Names are another area where you will find differences. There were, for example, several Ediths – Edward's queen, Harold's handfast wife, and his 'Roman wife' – and they are variously referred to as Edith, Edyth, Aldytha, Svana and even Richenda. We considered standardising such names but decided that these variations are part of the colour and fun of our little-known period of history, and represent each author's personal preference, so we let them stand.

After all, this is a collection of 'alternative history' stories where what we know, what we have imagined, and what we have shamelessly and joyously invented all meld.

We very much hope you enjoy the result.

Joanna Courtney
2021

JANUARY
1066

*O*n January 5th, after an illness – most likely one or more strokes – that had gripped him throughout the Christmas period, King Edward of England died. On his deathbed he was reported to have commended Harold of Wessex to the throne and certainly the Witan (high council) elected Harold to the role. He was crowned King the next day, January 6th, immediately after Edward's funeral.

England was content to be ruled by the man who had been named for the last few years as 'sub-regulus' (underking) and who had long controlled England's military defence. But in Normandy Duke William reacted with fury as he believed he had been promised England way back in 1051. Meanwhile over in Norway, Harald Hardrada, who had a tenuous claim from an old promise, started considering his options.

A tumultuous year was beginning for England…

TO CROWN A KING
Helen Hollick

Based on chapters taken from *Harold the King* (UK title)
I Am the Chosen King (US title)

*King Edward, later known as 'The Confessor' died on 5th
January 1066, just days after his Abbey of Westminster was
dedicated to God. Within hours, his Earl of Wessex, Harold
Godwinson, was crowned King of England – in unseemly haste,
the Normans later claimed. Not so, Edward's earls and nobles
had been at the Christmas Court for many weeks and wanted to
return to their lands, the next opportunity for a crowning would
not have been until Easter. The 'haste' was perfectly normal for
English law and custom.*

*The Normans also claimed that the childless Edward sent
Harold to Normandy in the 1060s to offer the crown to William.
This would have been highly unlikely: the English earls would
not have sanctioned it and it was for the Witan, the Council, to
elect a king – usually the eldest son, but it could be the man most
worthy to do the job. And there was already a legitimate heir,
Edgar, the young grandson of Edward's half-brother, Edmund
Ironside. In 1066, Edgar was only about thirteen years of age…*

Westminster, London – January 1066

The fifth day of January. For the first occasion in many a
week the sky had cleared and brightened from the misery
of rain, turning into the vivid blue of a clear winter sky.
There had been a nip of frost in the air during the day, but
as the sun had set, burning like liquid gold over the Thames
marshes, the temperature had dropped to below freezing.
Come morning, there would be a white crust riming the
edge of the river and the palace courtyard would be a film
of treacherous ice, cracking and snapping beneath
booted feet.

Throughout the short hours of daylight King Edward's breath had rattled in his chest, incoherent words flowing from his blue-tinged lips. His eyes fluttered open an hour before midnight, but they were dull within sunken hollows, and he did not seem to recognise any of the men gathered with grave solemnity around the bed. His wife, Edith, knelt at his feet persisting in her attempt to rub warmth into his lower limbs. Quiet tears drizzled down her pale cheeks.

'My lord?' Archbishop Stigand bent over him, not seeming to notice the fetid breath. 'You must make confession.'

Edward stared back; an empty soul fading away behind empty eyes. When he spoke, his feeble voice whispered from dry lips; 'Is my abbey complete?' he asked, his bone-thin fingers reaching out to pluck at the archbishop's woollen cloak.

Harold, Earl of Wessex, standing on the opposite side of the bed took Edward's left hand, raised it to his lips and kissed the royal ring that swivelled there, loose and over-large. 'Aye, my sweet lord, it is. We held the service of dedication yester-eve. Your Abbey of Westminster is consecrated.'

Edward nodded, a weak smile playing at one corner of his mouth. 'That is good,' he said, repeated, 'that is good.'

He closed his eyes again, lay there silent save for the shallow, rattling, breath. Then his eyes snapped open again, a brightness burning within them that had not been there before. 'I am for God,' he declared. 'I have no fear of meeting Him, I look forward to sitting at His feet. Bury me within my mausoleum, now it is made ready for my coming.'

Stigand nodded. 'There is no need to fear death, for you have served God well, and you go to an everlasting life from this transitory one.'

'The succession,' Edith hissed, rising to her feet and grasping the archbishop's arm, her fingers pinching through his vestments. 'Quick man! While he is lucid, ask him of my brother Tostig's forgiveness and the succession!'

. Harold, her eldest brother, remained silent. Had to admit to himself that his spoiled and selfish only sister was at least resolute, even if she held no other redeeming features. She was the childless Queen of England, and had never made secret her favouritism of their younger brother, Tostig. Not even when he had almost caused civil war in the North, had insulted King Edward to his face, and then fled abroad in disgrace. Not even all that had convinced Edith that Tostig, exiled Earl of Northumbria, could never, would never, be named as king after Edward no longer had need of his crown.

Either Stigand deliberately misunderstood her, or had no intention of mentioning Tostig's exile, a subject that would inevitably upset Edward. The archbishop stroked the back of the monarch's hand, said, 'We are here, my lord, we are at your side.'

From across the bed Edith glowered at Harold, furious that he had not demanded Edward reinstate their brother as earl, or gone into exile with him. Too wrapped in her own fear and disappointment to recognise the truth, she had refused to listen to Harold's insistence that Tostig's ineptitude had been the reason for the upset.

'No, no! Remind him of Tostig!' Edith hissed, brushing Stigand aside and taking her husband's hand earnestly within her own.

Irritated, Stigand indicated that Harold should say something.

To Harold, the eldest living son of the Godwins of Wessex, the commander of the English armies, and the most powerful man beneath the king, it did not seem possible that Edward was dying, that so much was going to change from this day forward. As a king Edward had fallen short of expectation, was almost as useless as Æthelred the 'Unraed', his father before him, yet unlike his father, the people loved Edward. His unstinting care and concern for the well-being of the common folk was commendable, as was his dedication and unwavering love for God. Not for the first time did Harold think that the man should have become a monk. As an abbot he would have been without fault – even down to his lack of duty in siring a child. To the best of Harold's knowledge Edith remained as innocent of a man as she had been on her wedding day. Edward himself had once, in a moment of drink-filled weakness, revealed that he had not managed to perform, that the both of them had remained virgin-pure throughout the many years of their marriage. The fault had been his, not Edith's – that too, he had acknowledged. The mystery remained, in Harold's mind, whether that fault was because of piety, natural impotence, or a secretive preference for intimacy with men.

Given Edward's outpouring of grief at Tostig's betrayal, Harold even wondered if his brother had been the object of Edward's base desires. Edward had been most fond of the young man, but to what extent? If there had been more than brotherly affection then Tostig was more the bastard than Harold had previously given him credit for. An intimacy of that nature would have been nothing but manipulative fraud on Tostig's part. Perhaps a more astute king would have urged caution in the North, or removed Tostig from office before it had been too late – but Edward was not a wise man. Ah, what was woven could not, now, be unravelled.

For his own part, Harold had never felt anything but courteous indifference towards Edward, neither liking nor disliking him. There were traits he admired, others he despised, but that was so of any man. None save Christ himself was perfect.

Harold sighed with regret for what might have been. He supposed there was room inside the hearts of some men for one area of excellence only. For Edward, it had been in his worship of God and the building of his splendid abbey. He stared at the sunken face beneath the white, silken beard, the blue eyes that sparkled, not with a zest for life, but from the heat of fever, *ðæt wæs göd cyning* – he was a good king. Harold sighed again. He could not deny Edward that epitaph, though it was not the full truth. It was not Edward's fault that he had made errors of judgement along his way, that he had been weak where he ought to have been strong. Edward had not wanted the weighty responsibility of a crown.

'There is much I need say!' Edward rasped. 'Are my earls and men of import around me?' He glanced fretfully at the occupants of the room.

Edith bit her lip; perhaps this was it after all? He was to forgive Tostig! 'They are all here, my dear husband,' she said, squeezing his hand, forcing a brave smile to her grief-gaunt face.

Satisfied, Edward continued with dignified clarity reciting the words of the *verba novissima*, the will declared aloud on the deathbed, naming lands and gifts that were to go to those who had served him well. He spoke of the loyalty his wife had shown him, stating that he had loved her like a daughter. He smiled up at her, begging her not to weep. 'I go to God. May He bless and protect you.'

In vain, Edith attempted to stifle a flood of tears and a conflict of surging emotions. *Like a daughter? The silly old fool should have loved me like a wife, like the mother of his children, not like a daughter!* She gulped more tears down; all these years she had felt little for Edward, had endured his presence, his whining and pathetic weaknesses, but suddenly, now she was to lose him, realised that she had looked upon him, this man who was three and twenty years her senior, not as a husband, but as a father. Did she love him? No, but she would miss him. Her tears fell.

Similar tears were pricking in the eyes of them all. Some men sank to their knees, others bowed their heads. All gathered there in that hot, fuggy, death-smelling chamber murmured the prayer of the Lord.

'My lord,' Stigand said softly, again leaning nearer to Edward who had closed his eyes, 'we would know your last wish. Would know who it is you would commend to follow you.'

Edward's eyes opened. He fluttered his left hand towards Harold. 'My Earl of Wessex.' Tiredness was creeping over Edward. 'I commend my wife's protection to Harold.' The effort of putting thought and speech together had taken everything from him. 'Leave me,' he gasped. 'I would make my confession.'

They left Edward's chamber, quiet and subdued. Death was always a sober reminder that an end must come for all, be they peasant, earl or king. Only Edward's personal priest remained; with reluctance, Edith went to her bower, grief cutting to her heart. She knew the rest would go to the council chamber to discuss the practicalities of her husband's death – the funeral, the succession. Tears and breath juddered from her. Her life had been so pointless, so utterly and completely pointless! Oh, if only Tostig had not been so stupid! If only Harold had supported him… If only, if only. Where did those useless words end? If only Edward had been a husband to her, had planted his seed within her. If only she had borne a child…

The murmur of conversation was low within the council chamber, flickering in unison with the draught-disturbed candle flames. All but a few of the Witan were present. Nine and thirty men. Two archbishops: Stigand of Canterbury and Ealdred of York. The bishops of London, Hereford, Exeter, Wells, Lichfield and Durham; among the abbots, the houses of Peterborough, Bath and Evesham.

Shire reeves and thegns, royal clerics, the king's chancellor... and the five Earls of England: Harold, his brothers Leofwine and Gyrth, and Eadwin and Morkere of the North. They talked of the morrow's expected weather, the succulence of the meat served for dinner, the ship that had unexpectedly sunk in mid-river that very morning. Anything unrelated to the difficulties that lay ahead in these next few hours and days.

Archbishop Ealdred stood and cleared his throat. 'My lords, we must, no matter that it is hard to do so, discuss what we all shy from.'

The light talk faded, grim faces turned to him, men settled themselves on benches or stools, a few remained standing.

'It is doubted that Edward will survive this night. It is our duty, our responsibility, to choose the man who is to take up his crown. I put it to you, the Council of England, to decide our next king.' Ealdred folded his robes around him and sat.

Those present were suddenly animated; opinions rose and fell like a stick of wood bobbing about on an incoming tide. Only two names were on their lips: Edgar, the boy ætheling, and Harold.

The two in question sat quiet on opposite sides of the chamber: one asking himself if this was what he wanted; the other, bewildered and hiding his fear. Edgar had never before been summoned to attend the council. It was not a thing for a boy not yet three and ten years of age, this was the world of men, of warlords and leaders. He looked from one to another, listened to snatches of the talk. Earlier that evening he had been immersed in a game of *taefl* with his best friend – had been winning. One more move... and they had come, fetched him away to sit in solemnity in that foul-smelling chamber with a dying man. Curse it! Sigurd always won at *taefl*; it had been Edgar's one chance to get even…! He stifled a yawn. Fought against closing his eyes to doze.

For an hour the men debated. Occasionally someone would toss out a sharp question to the boy, who startled awake, or to Harold, seeking opinion, assurance. Edgar answered as well he could. Harold with patient politeness.

The hour of two was approaching; servants had come and replaced the beeswax candles with new ones. The same words were passed around and around.

'As I see things,' Stigand said, his voice pitched to drown the rattle of debate, 'we have talked of but two contenders. Edgar?' He beckoned the lad forward. He came hesitantly, not much caring for this direct focus of attention for he was a shy boy.

Stigand continued, not noticing the reluctance. To be king was a thing sanctioned by God, personal feeling did not come into it. 'He is of the royal blood, but not of age. Second, Harold of Wessex.' Again the archbishop paused to motion the man forward. 'He has ruled England on Edward's behalf these past many years and has proven himself a wise and capable man, but there is a third possibility. Duke William of Normandy may claim the crown through the blood-tie of King Edward's lady mother, Queen Emma – God rest her soul – and through some misguided impression that Edward did once offer him the title.'

Immediately there were mutterings, shaking of heads, tutting. Upstart Norman dukes were unanimously declared as not understanding the civilised ways of the English.

Stigand half smiled, said, 'I take it, then, that William is excluded from the voting?'

'Aye.'

'That he is!'

'Damned impudence, if you ask me! The man is a bastard-born.'

The clerk at his table to one side was scribbling hastily,

9

attempting to write down as many of the comments as he could; the records would be rewritten later in neat script, the irrelevancies deleted, the gist of the proceedings tailored to fit the church-kept – and censored – chronicle.

'Duke William cannot be so easily dismissed,' Harold interrupted. He waited for the babble of voices to quieten. 'He is a bastard in more than birth alone. He will not heed anything said in this room, no matter how scornful or vehement. If he has set his mind on wearing a crown, then he will attempt to take it. If he is rejected, the question will not be if, how, or can he attack us, but *when*.'

He stood beside Stigand, saying nothing more. It was not his place to influence council, but it was difficult to keep his tongue silent with some of these more inane remarks. Duke William looked at things with a view distorted to match his own expectations.

The door to the chamber opened, heads turned, speech faded. Abbot Baldwin entered, his expression of grief telling his message. Archbishop Ealdred spoke the words of a prayer. 'Amen,' they all murmured.

'We are agreed, then?' Stigand said after a pause for reflective silence, 'Our King, Edward Æthelredson, may he rest at peace, commended his wife, our good Lady Edith, into the care of the Earl of Wessex. It is in my mind, heart and soul that he intended for Harold Godwinson to protect and reign over England.'

There came a murmur of disapproval from Morkere, Tostig's replacement as Earl of Northumbria.

'It is in my mind that Earl Harold, once crowned, may restore his brother to favour. I have no intention of relinquishing my earldom to that traitor.' He spoke plain. His brother, Eadwine, close at his side, nodded. Several thegns and nobles from the north agreed also. A bishop too, Harold noticed.

He stepped forward, offering his hand to Morkere. 'My brother is a jealous fool. I make no secret of the fact that I would rather have him in England, where I can keep an eye on him, but he will never return to Northumbria. You have my sworn word.'

Morkere did not take the proffered hand. 'Is your word good, my lord Earl? Did you not grant your word – your oath – that you would support William of Normandy in his claim for England?'

An uneasy silence. Harold smiled laconically. Morkere showed signs of becoming a worthy man to hold Northumbria.

'That oath,' Harold said, 'was taken under duress. I am under no obligation to keep it. When I visited Duke William, in all good faith, two years past, I was tricked into the choice of losing my honour or my life and freedom, and that of the loyal men with me. There are oaths, and oaths, my friend.' He nudged his hand further forward, inviting Morkere to take it, still smiling. 'I made that vow knowing full well that it was more dishonourable for a lord to endanger the lives of those who willingly followed him, than to pledge an oath with no intention of keeping it. I make this one to you, though, with a view to the opposite.'

Aware he had to give some other assurance to convince this rightfully suspicious young man, Harold added, 'Within our traditional law there is no dishonour in breaking a promise to a man who is himself dishonourable. To those who are worthy 'tis different.' For a third time he offered his hand. 'Take my word, Morkere, Tostig will not have Northumbria while I am able to prevent it. I give that unbreakable vow to you, a man I call worthy to receive it.'

Morkere was tempted to look at his brother, seek his opinion, but did not. He was his own man, with his own decisions to make – be they right or wrong.

Decisively, with an abrupt nod of his head, gazing steadily into Harold's eyes, he set his broad hand into the other man's.

'I accept your pledge, my Lord of Wessex.' Corrected

himself. 'My Lord King.' There was no need for Morkere to add anything further, for Harold understood the look that accompanied that acceptance from steady, unblinking eyes: *God protect you, though, should you break that oath.*

Harold stepped back, took a deep breath into his lungs. 'Before we decide about kingship, we should hear from the boy.' He trundled Edgar forward. 'Lad, tell us why we should crown you as our king?'

There came a few grumbles complaining of a waste of time, but several more of, 'Aye, let the boy speak!'

Edgar looked steadily up at Harold, gathering courage. He could say nothing, shrug, walk away, leave the chamber and this kingdom behind him. Instead, as had Harold, he took a deep breath.

'My grandfather was Edmund, known as Ironside. He was half-brother to the gentle king we have just so sadly lost to God. My grandfather died from mortal wounds inflicted in battle against the Dane, Cnut. For fear of his life by the hands of the new King of England, my father, then but a babe in arms, was taken into exile. He knew no palaces or comforts, had no sumptuous gowns or golden crowns. Instead, he knew the city of Kiev and the lands of Poland and Hungary. He grew, took a wife, had two daughters and a son.'

He paused, looked around at the men steadfastly listening to him. 'My sister, Margaret, is betrothed to Malcolm of Scotland, she will become a queen one day. My other sister, Cristina, wishes to serve God as a nun. I see her as abbess,' he paused, smiled, 'for she is most deft at organising and being bossy.'

The men laughed.

'Go on,' Harold murmured.

'I recall things from my childhood. Hearing the wind moan through the eaves of our rude-built house. Watching the snow fall. My father's footsteps making deep tracks in the blanketing whiteness as he went out to search for food, and wood for the fire. I recall huddling together at night and my mother burning the furniture to keep us from freezing. I remember the sun of summer days, so hot you could not talk or breathe.'

'This is all very well, an interesting tale, lad,' someone said from the back, 'but it does not make you the stuff of a king.'

Edgar lifted his chin, 'Does it not? Uncle Edward was not the stuff of being a king when he returned from exile in Normandy. My father, when Harold, here, escorted him – us – home to England would not have made a suitable king either, yet, had he still lived, would we be having this discussion? He would have been king by right of birth. I am his son. I am the last in the blood-line of Cerdic of Wessex, why then, should I not be your king?'

Someone, a bishop, laughed. 'Mayhap it has to do with you being a mere boy?'

He had found his courage now, and beyond all else Edgar suddenly realised that he wanted that crown. 'Boys grow into men. I know how to read and write – unlike the Duke of Normandy who cannot sign his own name. I speak more languages, probably than all of you men together in this room.'

'Aye, lad,' that was Earl Morkere, 'but you cannot fight. When William the Bastard comes, England will need to fight.'

Edgar hooked his thumbs through his belt, spread his legs slightly into a stance of authority. 'Mayhap I do not,' he answered, 'but neither did King Edward, yet no one gainsaid his crowning. And is that not what, you, the earls and advisors are for? I would hold the helm, you would sail the ship.'

There came a few ragged cheers, some impressed nods.

'Add to that, I have, as yet, no betrothed wife. I would send an emissary to broker a marriage between myself and one of Duke William's daughters. Were he to fight us, there is every chance he could sacrifice all; his duchy, his life. As father of the Queen of England he would have much to gain, and win.'

A few men applauded, more were nodding, agreeing.

'And last,' Edgar said, 'I have one advantage over all of you, including the Duke, and Earl Harold.' Again, he paused for effect. 'I know how to survive, and those who know that can be dangerous people – because we know we can do it.'

The chamber erupted into cheering. Harold grinned, knelt at Edgar's feet, smiled up at him.

'I offer my services, my lord, I would be proud to be Earl of Wessex for England's King Edgar.'

Rouen, Normandy, February 1066

The messenger refused to hand the letter sent from England to Duke William. Instead, he sought Fitz Osbern.

'But this is for the Duke. Why have you brought it to me?' Fitz Osbern was irritated. Naught had gone right this day – before leaving his bed he had quarrelled with his wife, then he had discovered his favourite hound had been in a fight during the night, sustaining a torn ear and tooth-gouged neck. Added to that, indigestion was burning in his chest – and now this fool was standing there hopping from foot to foot, proffering a parchment that was meant for Duke William. Pah! As if he did not have enough of his own correspondence to see to!

At least the messenger was honest in his reply.

'My lord, I bring it to you because it contains bad news. I have no intention of being on the receiving end of his temper.'

William Fitz Osbern sat at his table, letters spread before him, a quill pen leaning from the inkwell, shavings from other trimmed quills brushed into a neat pile. He stared at the scrolled parchment in his hand. It was from the Bishop of London. He sighed. Norman administration would be easier were their noble duke able to attend to the reading of charters and letters himself, and if the whole system were not so complicated. The recording of taxable land in England, for example, was much more organised, with everything meticulously written down and recorded in one book within each shire.

'If it is about King Edward's health, then we are aware he is failing. We are expecting to hear he is dead.' Will held the scroll out to the messenger. 'You have my assurance he will not bark at you for that.' Mint leaves would be good for his bubbling stomach. Perhaps he ought to send a servant to fetch some?

The messenger took a step backwards, emphatically refusing to take the document. ''Tis not the bark that concerns me, 'tis the sharp-toothed bite!'

Fitz Osbern suppressed a belch. 'For the sake of God, man, you have been paid to deliver a message to Duke William. Do so.' Fitz Osbern tossed the scroll at the man, who made no attempt to catch it.

'Nay, 'tis not my place to disagree, but I were commissioned to fetch this to Normandy. That, I have done. No one said anything about taking it direct to the man himself.'

Exasperated, Will heaved himself from his stool and fumbled for the scroll which lay among the floor rushes. 'I assume this great reluctance of yours is connected with the knowing of what is contained within this scroll?'

'*Oui.*'

'Which is...?'

The messenger scratched his nose. Ought he tell?

'Which is that the King of England is dead, and that Edgar Ætheling is crowned and anointed in his place.'

Fitz Osbern's grip tightened rigid around the parchment. Slowly, very slowly, he straightened. 'Repeat that.'

The messenger did so.

Fitz Osbern walked back to his stool, feeling as if he were ploughing through knee-deep mud. He could imagine the words written on the scroll burning through. Someone would have to read them aloud to Duke William. His indigestion paled into insignificance as a different kind of sickness rose into his throat. He nodded at the messenger. 'You may go.'

Relieved, the man fled.

Duke William sat very still. Only the slow, systematic rubbing of his thumb brushing across the ruby in his ducal ring, and the tight clench of his jaw, indicated his fury. 'Read it again,' he snapped.

Fitz Osbern reluctantly complied. Duke William's lips parted slightly, his nostrils flared. The thumb stopped moving.

The chamber was not crowded, but all within exchanged furtive glances of apprehension. Both servant and knight alike knew to beware of their duke when a rage threatened.

Duchess Mathilda, seated beside her husband, flicked a glance from the pale-faced Will Fitz Osbern to her husband and moved to rest her hand on William's arm. With irritation he jerked away. The abrupt movement broke the stillness. He lurched to his feet. He was a tall man – in anger, his stature seemingly heightened. His words, however, were low: 'And did Harold, Earl of Wessex, not speak on my behalf, as he swore to so do?

'*Non*, my lord.' Fitz Osbern allowed the scroll to roll up on itself, 'he did not.'

'He swore to speak for me, to convince the English of my claim.'

Fitz Osbern made no answer. There was none to make.

William clenched his fists, the nails digging into the

palms.' He swore. He took an oath before me, before God.' The words were becoming slurred, spoken through that rigid jaw.

Mathilda rose and put her hand over her husband's fist, was surprised to find that he was shaking. She too could not believe that what was written in that letter was the truth. Harold had seemed such a pleasant man, so benign – so honourable. She felt a blush tingle her face as she remembered him from his visit to Normandy; his laugh, those vivacious, enticing, blue eyes… Ashamed at a flurried erotic memory, she stifled the knot that was tangling her stomach and peered up at her husband. 'My lord, you are a greater man than ever this boy, Edgar, will be.'

Had William heard? His anger was swamping him, penetrating his senses, thundering in his brain. He had been betrayed before. Other men had sworn allegiance and reneged upon their oath. And other men had paid the price of their duplicity.

'He swore to speak my claim! He *swore*! Is this how England repays my kindness?' Resentment spewed from William's mouth. 'I welcomed him as a guest. I treated him as if he were one of my allies, offered him my confidence and friendship!' He lunged forward, scattering goblets, jugs and food bowls from a table, tipped the table itself. Struck out at a servant, clawed at a wall hanging and ripped it down. A few of the women screamed, men drew back, several dogs began to bark.

'He swore to make me King of England!'

Knowing no one else would attempt to calm him Mathilda intervened, her hands grasping his flailing arms. She was so small against him, her head barely reached his chest. She gripped tighter, shaking him. There were more than a few in that hall who secretly admired her bravery.

'It is done, husband. The thing is finished. Forget England. Forget it.'

William stared down at her, his expression a vice of

hatred. 'Forget England?' he said ominously. 'On the day I wed you, I promised you would not think of me as an illiterate barbarian, I promised I would prove my worth and strength, that I would give you a crown.'

Interrupting him, Mathilda declared, 'There is no need to prove anything, I have all I wish for. A husband who is loyal to me, who has given me handsome sons and beautiful daughters.'

Her words did not penetrate his mind.

'I vowed that I would make you my queen. And a queen, madam, you will be.' William pulled away from her, swung towards Fitz Osbern. 'So, this English whoreson, Harold, wishes to challenge my intention, does he? He has knelt before a boy and shouted 'God Save the King', has he? Well, we shall see what strength a spot-faced, beardless boy and an oath-breaking liar can muster against Normandy. I want England, and I shall have it. I *shall* have it!'

Mathilda went back to her chair, taking the letter from Fitz Osbern as she passed, offering him a smile of grateful thanks. Dare she tell her husband that she had no desire to be a queen, no care for England with its damp mists and drizzling rain? She sighed, read the letter for herself. This boy, Edgar, had every right to be crowned as a king. The proposal he offered seemed generous, and most suitable. She looked towards her young daughters standing subdued and silent to one side of the hall.

'Would this not,' she said tentatively, 'be a good match for our eldest daughter, our beautiful Agatha?'

William stared at Mathilda with cold disdain, the corner of his top lip curling in rage. 'You would have me,' he hissed, 'be made to look the fool?' He took a step towards her, his fist raised. To her credit, she did not flinch. 'You would have me,' the snarl increased, 'be of a lesser rank than a *girl*?'

Mathilda bowed her head, murmured, 'I apologise, I am a mere woman, what do I know of these political things?'

She looked up, smiled. 'Forgive me, you will make a superb king.'

As her husband turned away she retained the smile, but thought, '*Unless someone manages to do away with you first.*'

AUTHOR'S NOTE

Edward commended his wife, Edith, to her brother, Earl Harold's care – which was assumed that he also meant England. Harold did swear an oath to Duke William when he was in Normandy a few years earlier, (although we do not know *why* he was there,) but swearing false oath was less dishonourable, to the English, than endangering the lives of loyal followers. An oath made under duress was then, nor now, a binding oath – even Duke William knew that. (Although the Normans conveniently disregarded this fact.) From Harold's perspective, had he not sworn it is likely that he and his men would not have seen England or their freedom again – or even kept their lives. What would you have done in his position?

William claimed that Edward had promised him the throne. Was that likely? Edward was exiled to Normandy from 1016 to 1042 – a long time. He would have known the Duke as boy and man. His mother, Queen Emma, wife to King Æthelred, Edward's father, had abandoned Edward's care to her Norman relatives when she married the conquering Dane, King Cnut, in order to retain her position and crown. Perhaps Edward felt some obligation of gratitude to Normandy?

However, this 'promise' could only have happened in the early 1050s when the Godwin family were briefly out of favour and exiled. They clawed their way back because Edward was too friendly with the Normans, and the remaining English earls were not happy. They preferred the powerful Godwins, over ruthless Normans.

As for Mathilda's secret thoughts; far-fetched? Maybe

not, several years later she backed her eldest son in rebellion against William.

Helen Hollick
www.helenhollick.net

DISCUSSION SUGGESTIONS

If King Edward had officially, in recorded document, named Duke William as his heir, how would that have affected the events of 1066?

Did it matter to the ordinary people of 1066 who became king?

FEBRUARY

1066

*S*ometime after his coronation King Harold toured the north of England, looking to gain the loyalty of his subjects under Edwin, Earl of Mercia and Morcar, Earl of Northumbria, both young men. Edwin had inherited Mercia when his father, Lord Alfgar, died in 1062 and Morcar had been 'invited' to rule Northumbria by rebels who had cast out Tostig, brother of King Harold, in October 1065.

The North had traditionally been the least loyal part of the English kingdom. Far from the main seats of power in Winchester, Westminster and even Gloucester, they were a proud and determined people who could be a law unto themselves. Securing an alliance with the Northern earls was vital for Harold if he was to keep the country united against possible invaders. But how to do that?

Edwin and Morcar had a sister: Edyth of Mercia was still young but already the widow of King Gruffydd of Wales, to whom she had been married by her father in 1055. When Gruffydd, whose favourite pastime was harrying the English marches, had finally been driven to death by Harold and the English army in 1063, she had been brought back to England and in 1066, was the perfect vehicle, willing or otherwise, to unite North and South.

Records are not specific about when the wedding took place. It was certainly before either Hardrada or William landed and it was vital to Harold, for the men of the north held one of the main keys to keeping England safe in 1066...

A MATTER OF TRUST
Annie Whitehead

Wearing the crown is one thing, but if Harold were to rule with any security and authority, he needed the support of the northern earls. At some point between his coronation and April 16th, he travelled north to try to secure that support. It has often been said of Earl Morcar that he 'owed' his earldom to Harold, who had endorsed him after Tostig had been ousted.

The Earldom of Mercia had once been a separate kingdom, and nationalist fervour had often caused problems for the kings of Wessex. Mercia had strong links with the neighbouring Welsh, and Edwin's family had been close allies of Gruffudd of Gwynedd, whose death was engineered by Harold. Edwin and Morcar's grandfather had been a political rival of Harold's father, and the Godwin family had caused their father, Aelfgar, to be removed first from an earldom in East Anglia and then, briefly, from Mercia. These two families had 'history.'

Late February – York

The message, when it arrived, had been simple. *Edward dead, Harold is king. Come north.* Riding to answer his brother's call, Edwin had his grandmother's words still ringing in his ears. 'Our time has come, now. It is time to make Mercia great again.'

His gloves offered protection from the chilly air, a remnant of the winter that was slow to depart, but now he took them off, feeling the reins pressing into his palms while he stared at the leather embossing on his pommel. He had thought for a long time before setting out and was not convinced, even now, that he had done the right thing, not least because of the stench from the River Ouse assaulting his nostrils.

Opportunistic stallholders had set up along the roadside, breads and fresh spring cheeses laid out on rickety tables, but a baker with forearms as thick as Edwin's calves shook his head in disappointment when they rode past.

'It's the Mercians. Lord Edwin will have provisioned for them well enough. We'll have no sale today.'

They rode through the southern gateway of the erstwhile Viking kingdom of York, where the base of the stone watchtower was strewn with flowers, and had to slow their pace to avoid the press of people, brought out by the late winter sunshine and the presence of the King. Edwin swallowed against his Mercian revulsion to all things Norse; the odd, cellared buildings, the women wearing Norse-style silk caps instead of veils, the men with plaited and tied hair that resembled horse tails. The Godwins. Harold Godwinson was standing outside the Earl's hall, with members of the northern nobility, among them Oswulf of Bamburgh, and Edwin's brother, Morcar, the present Earl of Northumbria. Edwin dismounted and handed his reins to a waiting horse-thegn.

His younger brother came running to him, grinning wide enough to split his face. The afternoon sun shone on his hair. It had already left its mark on his face, where a band of fresh red covered his nose and the upper part of his cheeks. Despite the chill, he was in his undershirt. There was a slash in the sleeve; even today, Morcar had been in the yard, practising his sword skills. Oswulf followed him, and nodded at Edwin, before grasping his hand and drawing him in to pat his back. 'Welcome, Friend.'

Edwin had not seen Morcar for some months, but Morcar wasted no time on such greetings.

'Edwin, you must agree to Harold's kingship. Tostig was earl, and we threw him out. And when Tostig tried to take Northumbria back, Harold did nothing to help him. Think on it, he chose me as earl, over his own brother.'

Edwin sniffed. It wasn't much of a compliment. It was no ill reflection on Morcar, but Harold had simply chosen his only available option, as a condemned man might choose life instead of the gallows.

As if hearing his thoughts, Harold Godwinson moved away from the steps of Morcar's great hall. Moustaches neatly trimmed, carmine tunic blowing in the breeze, he descended with his unmistakeable swagger towards the newly arrived nobles, but Edwin could detect the doubt: the tilt of the head, the slump of his shoulders when the nobles he walked past refused to bow, instead folding their arms across their chests.

Harold stepped toward the Mercians, giving a slight wave of the hand held at hip level, an involuntary betrayal of his thoughts; that the opinions of those on the steps mattered less than those of the men he was approaching.

Behind Edwin, his friend Waltheof, lord of Southeast Mercia, slipped from his saddle and removed his gloves. He said, 'He only got where he is because his sister was married to the old king.'

Edwin turned to smile at his young companion. Son of

the old Northumbrian Earl Siward, Waltheof had been too young to succeed when his father died and thus Tostig had been appointed. Edwin never felt the wind on his back, for Waltheof was always there, loyal and dependable, and no friend to the Godwins. Edwin acknowledged his friend's remark with a pat on the arm. 'Wise words, as always.'

Waltheof returned the gesture. 'Do what you must.'

Oswulf said, 'Harold has a good sword arm. When Morcar made me lord of Bamburgh, he talked of how Harold dealt with the Welsh rebellion. In our fathers' day, he sailed with the Dublin men and I hear that he fought well on horseback with Duke William of Normandy two years ago.' As Godwinson approached, he added, 'But he will not hear it from me.'

Harold extended his arms as if he would embrace Edwin, but when Edwin kept his arms folded, he turned the gesture into one of query. 'What say you, Earl Edwin? You have taken a blessed age to get here. There is much we need to talk about.'

Morcar placed his weight on one leg and then the other, as if his bladder were full. 'Many men have tried and failed to get my brother to speak at length about anything, my lord.' His words were directed at Harold, but his gaze was fixed on his elder brother, the same beseeching expression that he'd used often, always deferring to Edwin after their father had died, too young.

Harold said, 'I know you don't trust me, but didn't I prove myself when I helped Morcar?'

Edwin looked at the older man. Let him say it. Let him acknowledge it. He gripped his sword hilt, pressing his flesh against the jewelled pyramid at the top, cool, unyielding. He would have to hang up his sword when they went inside, but for now it kept him stable, helped him plant his feet, stand steady, unwavering.

Harold spoke again, quickly, as if needing to fill the silence. 'I know your father had no love for me. Indeed, your grandfather had no love for my father. But England can be different now.' He touched a hand upon Edwin's forearm. 'Please, Lord Edwin, walk with me…'

April – London

'How could you?' A week had passed since Easter Sunday. Ealdgyth looked as if she had been crying since Good Friday.

Often Edwin had seen her with streaks on her cheeks, and with eyes rubbed red against salty tears, but this time the chin was down, the eyes wide in reproach. His sister need not speak; he knew.

But she continued. 'Dragging me to London on the pretence of seeing you bow down formally to Harold, and all along you had sold me to him as a bride. How could you, Brother? Not enough that he has made me a widow…'

'I could not help what was done to Gruffudd of Gwynedd. I was too young. Father thought…'

'You are not too young now! What of my children, the life I had carved for myself in Wales? I was young, too, when father sold me to Gruffudd. But I made the most of it. At least he was kind to me, and a friend to our family.'

She inhaled a ragged breath and paused, and he knew that she too could hear the scrape-click that announced their grandmother's imminent appearance.

Godiva came in to the hall from her private guest chamber beyond the great painted screen, leaning heavily on her carved stick, but keeping the jewel-encrusted tip visible, preserving the pretence that it was no crutch, merely a fashion accessory. The heavy gold and emerald cross, worn every day that Edwin could ever remember, swung across her chest with every step, and he took her elbow, ignoring her attempts to shake away his assistance as he led her to a chair. When she sat down, her head went forward, pushed these days by the hump at the back of her neck, but even though her eyes were shrunken by the years, they still shone speedwell blue and her brow, with every grey hair tucked severely under her veil, surrendered to barely a wrinkle.

Godiva glanced at Ealdgyth, cleared her throat, and fixed her gaze upon Edwin.

'Twice.' She nodded, and held up two fingers. 'Two times the Godwins forced my son into exile. Your own father; hounded out of his lands. With Gruffudd's help, he got his earldom back, but is it any wonder he died before his time?' Her voice cracked on the last word, turning it into two syllables. 'But that wasn't enough for Harold, was it? He bribed the Welsh to kill Gruffudd.' She sniffed, and then drew her lips together, hastily correcting herself as if she knew it would encourage wrinkles around her mouth. 'The Welsh were our protection against the grasping Godwins. I lived to bury my son, I've seen my granddaughter widowed, her children left fatherless.' She glanced at Ealdgyth, reaching out as if to pat her knee. 'And now you,' she glared at Edwin, 'now you make peace with Godwin's whelp? This is not what I prayed for when you went north; for you to give him your sister as soon as he asked.'

'He didn't ask. I suggested it.'

Ealdgyth made a sound like a wounded animal and ran from the room.

'What's that?' Godiva cupped her ear. 'Speak up?'

Edwin shook his head, declining to repeat it, and lifted his palms as if supplication might soften her resolve. 'She is the widow of one rebel; do you want her to be sister to another? Do not forget, when the northern earls rose against Tostig last year, Harold supported Morcar.'

In response, she harrumphed, falling back on the privilege of the elderly, making argument with disparaging noises. 'Ha! What were they thinking, giving Northumbria to a southerner in the first place?'

His silence seemed to convince her that he had no more argument for her. She grimaced as if trying to swallow curdled milk. 'Tostig is a disloyal son. His brother Svein abducted a nun. Harold widowed your sister. You willingly deal with such weasels?'

'Harold will not harm our sister.' The Godwin treated his hand-fasted woman, she of the swan neck, well enough. But Morcar was a swordsman, a fighter, not a deep thinker. 'Morcar says he owes Harold a debt.' He bowed low, and turned on his heel, saying, 'Let him believe it. For now.'

'Who? Let who believe it?'

He let the words hang in the stale room as he went in search of fresh air.

The roof space of the minster was filled with cloying incense smoke which seemed to dull the sound of the singing. Harold the King wore a floor-length tunic, with gold fabric at the edge of the neckline. His belt shone with inlaid garnets and rings sparkled on three fingers of each hand. Ealdgyth was wearing a blue shot-silk dress, its sleeves bordered with red. In contrast to Harold's close-fitting cuffs, her fingers barely showed beneath her wide sleeves. She was wearing a simple veil. They both wore soft leather slippers, but her dress was so long that only the toes of hers were visible. Despite already having been a bride, and having borne children, she looked small, vulnerable. There was no doubt that she was fertile, and would have more babies, but every time Edwin had seen her over recent years, she had had her children alongside her. Now, she was alone. Edwin swallowed hard.

Beside him, their grandmother was wearing a head cloth, wrapped many times. A dress of pale yellow sapped her elderly skin of all colour. Morcar was in a green tunic, his face washed and scrubbed so that his cheeks gleamed red. He looked like the rich earl that he was, but he sat slumped. Was the perceived debt pressing on his shoulders? The thought made Edwin sit up straight. Godiva's face was pinched, her mouth puckered in sour wrinkles, until she spotted him looking at her. She returned his sideward glance with a glare, and hissed, 'You should have told him.'

What could he have done? He thought again about the previous year's rebellion. He didn't need his grandmother to point out what he already knew: that Harold simply backed down in the face of Edwin's combined Mercian and Welsh army. Morcar didn't realise that he owed his earldom not to Harold, but to his elder brother. How could he humiliate him with the truth? He fixed his gaze on the Godwin. Harold reached up and smoothed his moustaches. Edwin thought of the cats sneaking out of the dairy, that preened in the sunshine of the yard and wiped the illicit milk from their whiskers.

With the days getting longer and lighter, the main meal was served later in the evening. The oil burned brightly in the wall-cressets and the heat from the hearth-fire was welcome; despite the longer days, the nights were still cool and fine wedding clothes were impractical for keeping out the chills of evening. The tables were laden with bread made from the finest sifted wheat. Spit-roasted lamb and kid meat was sliced and brought from the cooking fires, and servants poured the traditional bride-ale and the finest wine into gold cups. Carved wooden pillars supported the great oak roof, and the walls were hung floor to ceiling with embroidered panels worked with gold and scarlet thread. The noise of revelry filled the huge space and made conversation possible only with immediate neighbours.

Ealdgyth barely drank. Instead, she picked at the skin on the side of her thumbnail, a habit Edwin remembered from her childhood, when anguish or upset sent her to a quiet corner and saw her worrying away at her fingers, sometimes until they bled.

Morcar, sitting near her on the head table, applauded the glee-men who, having finished their dancing, bowed to make way for the scop. He filled his own cup instead of waiting for the servants to pour and shouted answers to the scop's riddles.

'I can think of other things made stiff by churning...' But the hand that poured the wine was tremulous; the earl who'd sworn allegiance to Harold was at odds with the man from Mercia with a family whose name he was desperate not to shame, and who made a study of the wood patterns on the table whenever his grandmother's flinty scowl flew in his direction.

Godiva, alternately wincing at his bawdy answers to the riddles, and glaring at Harold who sat with his coronet still upon his head, waved away all drink as if the West Saxon wine were poisoned

'Back in the days when such things mattered, London was part of Mercia, you know,' she said to anyone who was close enough to have to listen. 'My husband was a great man and I, well, did you know about the time that I...'

Edwin sat forward and placed his hand over hers. 'No, you didn't. It is a tale that grows with the telling, but the truth is you simply rode without your jewels on, and wearing a plain shift. Come, it is time you were abed.'

She said, 'What need have I for sleep, when you have stuck a knife through my Mercian heart,' but did not resist when he pushed back his chair and lifted her gently to her feet, even though she carried on muttering as they picked their way through the crowded benches, dodging any flailing arms that accompanied raucous story-telling.

'We were rich but pious. Your grandfather was well-loved, not like those barbarous Godwins...'

Edwin motioned to Morcar with a raise of the eyebrows and a sideward glance, and Morcar came round to her other side. Talking across her, they masked as well as they could her insults against their host.

Outside, the contrast between the noisy hall and the peaceful courtyard was more marked than usual. There was no sound of vomiting, or bladders being voided. None of the usual conversation, conducted in the yard between speakers who'd escaped from within in the hope of being heard. Folk who'd come from the wedding and those who were merely going about their business, were all standing still, and silent. Edwin followed their gaze upward to the stars and crossed himself.

Godiva clutched her crucifix and whispered, 'The saints preserve us.'

Edwin shouted the order to his horse-thegn that he was ready to leave. He shifted in his saddle and saw Morcar walking towards him, leading his stallion by the rein.

'You've made your mind up, then? You're not going to wait and wait, like you did when King Edward died?'

Edwin shook his head. There was nothing to consider. 'Tostig is becoming a bane. He must think that thing,' he jerked his head upwards, 'is lighting his way. This has naught to do with kingship, or loyalty. The bastard is on our lands, and he needs to be shoved off them.'

Morcar also looked up, to where the fiery-tailed star still shone, like a beacon sent from God Himself, even a week after the wedding. 'We ride to Lincolnshire, then?'

Tostig Godwinson was making a nuisance of himself and they had a duty to protect the people on their land. Edwin nodded. 'To Lincolnshire.'

Morcar jumped up and slapped Edwin on the back. 'That thing up there is a good omen. Our sister is wed to England's King, and God likes the idea. Now we will tell Tostig the good news, in a way that he might finally understand.'

Edwin sighed. There was one thing to consider, of course. The need to keep his enthusiastic brother from getting himself skewered on a Godwin spear. Tostig and Harold evidently did not agree, but blood was always thicker than water.

September – Fulford, outside York

This time, he could not respond to the message. *Belly round now with the child. Please bring Grandmother to me.* The harvest had been gathered less than a month ago and in three days folk would be celebrating the 'even night', the feast of Mabon, when day and night were equal in length, and beer and wine would be drunk in huge amounts in thanksgiving of the safe bringing in of the earth's bounties. His sister had been wed five months; by his reckoning he would be an uncle again come the new year. But Godiva could not be fetched to Ealdgyth, and once again, Edwin's heart tugged against the walls of his chest, as if pulling to be away from where his body had dragged it.

Tostig, defeated four months ago in Lincolnshire, had not learned his lesson but had marched, instead, on York. Edwin turned to look out across his own massed ranks. They stood between the enemy and the city, outside the gates of Fulford, shield wall ready, the ancient tribal banners slapping as the wind buffeted them. The reassuring *wubba-wubba* of the flapping flags reminded him that all the levies had answered his call, that he had enough northern fyrdsmen to carry the day. Behind them, inside the walls, the rumbling of the supply train cartwheels competed with the clanging of shields, weapons and shirts of mail still being unloaded. Pray God they would not need them.

He'd taken one last look at the sky before putting on his helmet. Pray also that he would not be staring up, unseeing, at that cloudless blue where carrion crows were already circling, at the day's end. They occupied the higher ground, giving them an additional advantage, even though the foetid aroma rising from the marshes made his stomach threaten its own rebellion. Tostig was not just a nuisance this time. This time he had the army of Harald of Norway standing alongside him. Reportedly, three hundred ships had sailed up the river until the invaders disembarked at Ricall ten miles to the south, but what he saw here belied that figure and Edwin's inclination was not to wait for the report to be proven. But was their advantageous position enough?

It was a Viking host, like the ones his forefathers had faced. Some had plaited their beards, but it was their equipment that marked them as foreign. Their shields were round, like those of the lower ranks in Edwin's army. He tapped his kite-shaped shield onto the ground; sturdy, protective. While the sun's reflection glinted off their axes, he carried his father's sword, as always, and his fingers curled round the hilt, embracing an old friend. Morcar, the younger son, had had his own sword forged and designed it with a disc-shaped pommel. He'd practised every day; now was a chance to test it in anger. Edwin sent up one final prayer, that he would be able to keep his brother safe during that first test.

Despite the turning of the season, sweat trickled down the nose plate of his helmet and pooled on his top lip. And then he saw Tostig. He knew him from the Godwin swagger, the manner of walking which all the sons had, legs apart, causing a sideward gait. He wore scarlet leg bindings over bright blue breeches. The Godwin was gathering his housecarls to him, positioning his personal guard in close formation. He was wearing a Norse-style helmet, with circles of metal around the eyes. It befitted his foreign origins.

You have stuck a knife through my heart.
How could you, Brother?
You're not going to wait and wait, are you?

33

The tugging in Edwin's chest was replaced with the relaxation of tension having snapped.

With the knowledge that Oswulf and Waltheof would follow, he gave the signal and charged toward the enemy. His men were either side of him but not in a formation that could be described as a shield wall. They slammed into the front ranks of Tostig's forces, who'd not had time to form the tight wall that would have protected them. Slashing with his sword, Edwin brought his blade down upon the necks of those who stood in his way, cleaving bodies from shoulder to belly. The roaring behind him told him that the English had followed him and he pushed on, until he caught sight of Tostig again. Slamming those who impeded him with a shove of his shield, he focused on the flash of blue with the crisscross of scarlet binding that identified his target. He tripped, but maintained his balance, and looking down and slightly back, he saw that it was not a rock but a severed foot which had caused him to stumble. His throat complained, rupturing from the screaming, but he yelled his death cry again and again as he hurtled towards the Godwin.

Tostig turned, his mouth opened, and then a housecarl stood in front of him, brandishing his axe. Edwin's vision was tinged now with the scarlet, even when he looked up. He blinked hard and fast, and bundled into the housecarl, deflecting the axe blow with his shield, swiping sideways with his sword and bringing it across the man's waist, all but severing torso from legs. Tostig stood transfixed. In a moment he would rally, but Edwin didn't wait. Lunging forward, he slashed at Tostig's legs, and as the Godwin went down, the Mercian blade cut across his neck. Head and helmet separated, and both thudded to the ground.

Panting, throat on fire, Edwin stood as the English fyrdsmen thundered past him. He saw Morcar, running towards the Norwegian contingent. In the melee, nothing could be discerned, but moments later the raven banner of Harald Hardrada disappeared from view. Edwin nodded his satisfaction; Morcar had killed the king of Norway.

As more of the invaders arrived, the English pushed them back towards the swampy ground, and the battle cries were replaced with the shrieks of men drowning in water too shallow to swim, too deep to allow breath. In the distance, troops arriving upon the battleground turned and fled. The morning sun had not reached its zenith and yet, the day was over.

Edwin stared at Tostig's body. The leg-bindings were now dark blood-red, wet from the marshy ground. How quickly brightness could fade. Now. Now was the time. Edwin exhaled, long and hard, as if he had been holding his breath since King Edward's death.

He turned to the touch on his shoulder. Morcar was standing behind him, hair sweated to his head, a gash on his cheek, but otherwise, whole.

'A message came. I could not tell you earlier. You were…' he looked down at the headless corpse, 'busy.'

Edwin's throat was still raw. To save his voice, he raised an eyebrow in enquiry.

'Duke William has landed an army in the south.'

The people of Fulford raised a cheer as the broken raven banner was dragged through the gate.

Morcar raised his voice. 'At least we have saved Harold a ride north.'

Would Harold have faced his brother on the battlefield? When it came to it, how thick was the Godwin blood? Edwin nodded. 'He will be fresh for battle with William.'

'Shall we go south?'

'No.' He had no more wish than the next man to fight two battles in quick succession. 'It's not our fight.'

Morcar frowned and wiped sweat from his brow. 'How can you say that? Harold fights for his crown, and for England. Is that not what we fought for here?' He circled his sword arm shoulder, massaging it at the joint. 'I owe him.'

Edwin shook his head. No, Harold owed them. And now that Tostig was out of the way, they didn't need Harold. For anything. 'We were fighting for our earldoms, and the folk who depend on us.'

Morcar looked up at him, eyes beseeching, as he appealed to his elder brother. 'And if I go?'

Harold would win against William. His prowess in battle was legendary and he had fought alongside William and knew his tactics. Morcar had survived his first battle, and fought well. Even with Harold's fighting skills, Morcar would be more than a make-weight in his army. 'You will be a useful sword arm for Harold.'

Morcar stood tall and his chest puffed out. 'And you? You mean not to support Harold? Then why did you bow down to him in the first place? What will you do?'

He would send for his sister, keep her safe, out of harm's way of the battle and its aftermath. *Why did you bow down?* Oh, how easy it would have been, to deny Harold, to make Godiva proud. But they needed royal backing until Tostig was out of the way. Edward's death had thrown the silver pennies in the air, and Edwin had guessed, accurately, where they might land. It had taken some time, but all had fallen into place.

She is the widow of one rebel; do you wish her to be the sister of another?

Now, whatever happened, Ealdgyth was a queen. Either she would be the mother of a king, or, well… *Harold only got where he is because his sister married the king.* If the babe turned out to be a girl, then why not the queen's brother, to rule in its stead?

Yes, that comet was a good omen, for it foretold Mercia once again in ascendance.

Morcar asked again. 'So, where are you going?'

To speak to the Welsh. 'To raise an army.'

Morcar shook his head and shrugged his shoulders in query. 'To fight William?'

'No.' Let Harold take care of William, the last of the contenders.

Edwin's thegns were beginning to gather. Edwin put his hands on his brother's shoulders and squeezed. Nodding to his men to follow, he walked off the battlefield towards his horse, mounted up, and gave the order to ride out.

Waltheof, riding beside him, said, 'Where to?'

'Home.'

Next time, when the message came, he would be ready.

AUTHOR'S NOTE

In reality, although Edwin did advance early at Fulford, he and Morcar were defeated. Their failure at the Battle of Gate Fulford forced Harold's march to Stamford Bridge, there to confront, and defeat, the combined forces of Harald Hardrada and Tostig Godwinson (and thus, of course, Harold did indeed face his own brother on the battlefield). Had the northern earls succeeded at Fulford, Harold would not only have had a fresh army, but Edwin and Morcar might have made it south in time to supplement that army, instead of arriving, as they did, after the decisive battle at Hastings, where in all probability the English would have defeated William.

Can we assume that the crown would have sat on Harold's head for very long after that?

History tells us that Morcar owed his earldom to Harold's refusal to support Tostig when the northern lords rebelled. We don't know exactly when Harold married Ealdgyth, but we do know that he felt the need to ride north some time after Edward died – in January – and that he was back in London for Easter on April 16th. (According to the Anglo-Saxon Chronicle, the comet appeared on 24th April.) Yet his brother Edwin had nothing to gain from supporting Harold and I wonder why he did.

There was a long-running and well documented feud between the two families. Earl Siward had been a friend of Leofric, grandfather to Edwin and Morcar and husband to Godiva. It's unlikely that his son, Waltheof, would have been loyal to the Godwins. I think he would have followed Edwin, as would all the northern lords. Morcar and Edwin were both conveniently nearby when the northerners rebelled and Harold backed down in the face of the combined Mercian and Welsh army.

Even if Harold survived Hastings, a precedent had been set: although in theory the Witan had always chosen the next ruler, the reality was that the king was always of royal blood, until Harold. Edwin's claim would have been at least as strong.

Annie Whitehead
www.anniewhiteheadauthor.co.uk

DISCUSSION SUGGESTIONS

If Harold had held onto the throne in 1066, would the Northern earls have, at some point, rebelled, or would being kindred to the next royal heir have been enough for them?

Why does England have such a deep-rooted and still strong North/South divide? Did the events of 1066 have an impact on that?#

MARCH
1066

*V*ikings, so their reputation would have it, were rarely slow to spot an opportunity for raiding or, indeed, conquest. Indeed their name probably derives from the phrase going '*i-viking*': raiding. The Scandinavians had been sailing forth on adventures for hundreds of years by the 11th century – even getting as far as America – and were very familiar with the short hop across the Northern Seas to England. Even in midwinter, it would not have taken long for news of King Edward's death to make its way to Norway where Harald Hardrada (meaning 'Ruthless') had been king for twenty years. It does not seem to have taken long, either, for him to decide to invade.

Sometime in early 1066 it seems that King Harald had a visitor to his royal court in Oslo – Tostig Godwinson, Harold's brother, who had been exiled in 1065 and was now looking for a way back into England. Tostig had almost certainly already been to the courts of William of Normandy and Svein of Denmark but, finding no ally there, was now trying his luck with Hardrada.

It seems unlikely that the King of Norway saw much benefit in the help of a lost English earl with only a handful of ships, but neither did he see much harm and he agreed to let Tostig join him. It is also possible that talking to him cemented Hardrada's own determination to invade. His claim to the throne was via a tenuous pact between Harthacnut, briefly King of England before Edward (he was Edward's half-brother by Queen Emma and King Cnut) and Magnus, King of Norway before Hardrada. The legal claim mattered little to a Viking though – what was important was winning in battle.

Hardrada had rarely lost a battle in his life. He was a rich and highly experienced warrior with an invasion force of some three-hundred ships full of eager and warlike Vikings, seeking to emulate the great King Cnut's successful invasion exactly fifty years before – he did not expect to lose...

EMPEROR OF THE NORTH
Joanna Courtney

Harald Hardrada, renowned Viking warrior and King of Norway, had two important 'right-hand men' – Lords Halldor and Ulf. They seem to have been with him from his early years as a Varangian mercenary and were a key part of his stable rule of Norway from 1047. Halldor returned to his homeland of Iceland in 1051, but Ulf remained as Harald's High Commander until he died in early 1066, just before the invasion of England.

Was it, I wondered, the lack of this level-headed commander that led to Harald making what must be one of the only tactical mistakes of his prestigious military career in turning up at Stamford Bridge with only half his army, and they not in full armour? This story, told by Aksel, imaginary son of Lord Halldor, explores that possibility and the effect it might have had on England if Norwegian Harald had defeated English Harold in 1066.

It was a fine year, 1066 – a year to be sung to the rafters of the mead halls, a year to hail the crowning of a mighty king: Harald Hardrada, Emperor of the North. Not that I ever doubted he would do it. None of us did, for had Cnut not done the same fifty years before, and he facing a king of royal lineage not a trumped-up earl trying his luck at a throne too big for his scrawny warrior's arse?

Harald had been a king long before 1066 and a fine one. They didn't call him Hardrada – Ruthless – for nothing. He'd won Norway in 1047 and held her for nigh-on twenty years before he challenged for England. I should know, for I was born in his war camp, son to his trusted friend Lord Halldor of Myvatyn, and was passed to Harald for luck as soon as my cord was cut. I followed him from that moment and my main memory of boyhood was the painful frustration of being parted from him, my father and their third great friend, Lord Ulf, when they sailed to war. I was first to volunteer, therefore, when Harald spoke of England for I did not wish to be left behind on this, his greatest adventure.

Let me introduce myself – Aksel Halldorson, Earl of Wessex and Commander of the King's troops either side of the Narrow Sea, though I am little use in that office these days, being more or less confined to my bed since the summertime of this year of our Lord, 1086. I am but two and fifty – almost the age Harald was in 1066 – but I have some damned disease that is wasting away my bones and no one, it seems, can do anything about it save coddle me with blankets and broths like an old-one.

I did drag myself up for the victory celebrations in October but even feasting wore out my silly brittle bones and I had to watch the dancing from the sidelines with the other cripples. I felt a fool all right, especially with our dear Emperor Harald still upright on his throne in Westminster's fine hall, his blond hair now purest white. But my heart still burned with pride to know that I had been there, exactly twenty years before, when he first took that throne, and the memories keep me going even now that I am almost done with this life.

'They said we were mad!' That's how my father used to tell the events of 1066. 'They said we could never take England, that she would be too strong for us – but we sailed on her anyway.'

He was always one for the drama in a tale, Lord Halldor, and he liked to make out the expedition was harder than it was, but in truth no one said that we were mad – they just said, 'show us the path'. Vikings, even these days, are ever keen to take to the whale road and men were summoning their crews the moment Edward died and Harald spoke of England. We were wild enough to yearn for battle and arrogant enough to believe we could seize England, the jewel in Europe's crown – a land so sure of itself that all men longed to hold it. Earl Harold longed, for sure, Duke William too, but God did not choose them. God chose Harald Hardrada of Norway and Harald has paid Him back with twenty years of security and prosperity for his people.

I think of it still sometimes, feel it even. That great year of 1066 creeps into my mind often these days – usually when dawn threads through my rich bed-hangings in whispers of light and the past feels every bit as real as the present to a man hovering on the edge of both.

'Invasion,' the men call to me still, as delighted as if it were a great feast they were being summoned to. 'Invasion. Conquest. Adventure.' Always adventure – even now that it is more in my fading mind than in my sword arm.

It was Queen Elizaveta, though, who really drove the mission, who yearned for the adventure of it. That's how Harald tells it and *that* is true. Believe me, I knew Elizaveta from 1035 when I was still a babe and she took me into her mother's royal nursery at Kiev so that I would not have to be carried from war camp to war camp with my father. I resented that sometimes as I grew older, but she was right to do it for I might never have made adulthood had she not and then I would not have been a part of this great Empire of ours. And oh, I loved her. She was scarcely more than a child herself at just sixteen but I thought her as beautiful a lady as in any of the legends told around the hearthfires and I devoted myself to her service.

I sat at her feet whenever I was allowed, and whenever she sat still, which was not often, for she was a woman with adventure in her veins. She was a true Viking queen for a true Viking king and still people call blessings upon her. Beautiful, fiery, exciting, she has brought Rus elegance to England. And through her sisters – married to kings throughout Europe – she has placed us at the heart of a great skein of trade routes that means that even now, as I clutch at the last golden threads of life, my days can be eased by fine fabrics on my back and rich foods on my plate. I can be blessed in churches glowing with the colour and fire of Byzantine artists. Yes, England is a better place for having Elizaveta as her queen.

I can see her now, riding the waves with us that burn-bright day in August 1066 when we turned our dragon prows out of Norway's Sognafjord and west towards England. She refused to be left behind in Norway and I believe she would have ridden all the way to York and into battle besides given half a chance for she was a fiery woman, God bless her. But Harald left her in the Orkneys with their daughters until he could safely summon her to the throne. It did not take long.

We did not expect it to be easy. We are not fools. Vikings are fierce but we are canny too. We do not win battles by madness, whatever others may conveniently think, but by cunning – by preparation and wise choices even in the heat of the moment. Wiser choices than the English, for it was their poor decision at Fulford that won us that first victory. Their commanders, the lords Edwin and Morcar were young and driven more by courage than experience. They will tell you as much themselves, for we laugh about it sometimes still, when we are all at court together.

It is hard to believe now, that we were once such bitter enemies. Edwin married Harald and Elizaveta's second daughter, Ingrid, the year after the conquest and they have given our king many grandchildren to run him ragged. They are gentle souls, both, and are happiest on their lands in Mercia and working to promote peace with Wales, which is no easy task even with Edwin's Welsh royal nephews in his care.

Morcar is less gentle. Always one with a sparkle in his eye, he enjoyed life as a conqueror for a year or two before he fell in love with a fearsome Norwegian girl who came over for Harald's magnificent coronation as Emperor in 1072. Ever since their wedding he has divided his time between Northumbria and Norway so that he has become, we tease him, more Norse than us Norse. I believe he sometimes sees his sister, the exiled nine-month-queen Edyth, and her son, Harold Haroldson, but no one speaks of them and the boy has never sought to challenge the Emperor of the North so we leave him be. But then, why would he? Only a fool would overthrow such a stable rule.

Thank the Lord, Edwin and Morcar ran from Fulford and thank Him again that they came out and submitted to us after Stamford Bridge, for they have been loyal servants and together we have made England stronger. Back in 1066, though, they were determined to see us from their shores. I can see them now, teeth bared, swords high, fury in their young eyes. They'd arrived at the battle-site first and set their armies tight against the marsh to force them to stand firm and fight. Harald commended their bravery but he knew how to exploit it too. All we had to do was to hit them hard and drive them sideways and let the suck and pull of the bog do the rest of the work.

I still hear that battle sometimes; it is perhaps the most vivid memory of them all. It had a peculiar sound as sword-wound cries gurgled into silence beneath the marsh water as if the earth itself had swallowed up the Saxons' pain. And there were so many of the fallen – so many that by the end you could run across even the soggiest sections of the battlefield on their backs. Many did, but not me. I was sickened by it. When I was younger, Elizaveta used to tease me that I was too soft for a Viking and she may be right but I see little joy in trampling the dead for we will all be gone one day. One day soon for me.

We took York undisputed. I'm not sure if her people were afraid of us or pleased to see us. Some were certainly the latter for there is much Norse blood in the north of England. It was the Northerners who welcomed Cnut when he conquered fifty years before us and, indeed, it was the Northerners who eventually saw us to Westminster once the usurping Earl Harold was dead. After Fulford though, that task was still ahead of us.

Harald was keen to secure York. He arranged for hostages and treasure to be delivered to us at a pretty meadowland around Stamford Bridge, a key meeting of the main roads across the district. It was such a hot day. I remember that well for the sweat felt as if it was running like a very river beneath my mail. I longed to take it off, we all did, and Harald might have let us – for what threat was a handful of cowed hostages? – but Ulf refused and Ulf was captain of the army and the king's friend since childhood, so he was allowed to overrule him.

'The men are boiling alive,' Harald said to Ulf.

I can hear him now, as if the pair of them were stood the other side of my bed-hangings. But Ulf was having none of it.

'Let them boil. A good Viking is always ready for battle.'

'There *is* no battle,' Harald laughed.

How wrong he was – not only was there *a* battle, but *the* battle, the one that won him the crown. And, oh, did he thank Ulf for his foresight when the English spears tipped the hillside! For it was Ulf, too, who had ordered almost the full force of our men to Stamford Bridge so that at that dread moment we outnumbered the arriving army. There had been much grumbling for it had been a long, hot walk from the ships at Ricall and men were keen to stay at the cool of the riverside, but Ulf had insisted.

'A good Viking is always ready for battle' he'd said then too, adding, 'we are on enemy territory and cannot be too careful.'

And thank the Lord he'd insisted for it was not a straggle of hostages that we met on that pretty field, but a vast army, marched all the way from London by King Harold.

He was a good man, King Harold, from all we saw. Am I sad he had to die? A little, perhaps, for the world needs good men, but war is war and he understood that as well as we. The bastard Norman duke ranted on about rights and oaths and sent off for a damned scrap of a papal banner to trumpet his claim, but Harold knew, as we knew, that this was nothing about 'right' and everything about power. It was an honest contest in that way and one we are proud to have won for Harold was a brave and determined general. I had to admire him for that. Harald admired him for it too. I remember his mouth falling open as he saw the 'fighting man' standard of the English king – a standard that should still, by rights, have been flying over Westminster.

'He is quite a man, your brother,' he said to Earl Tostig.

That didn't please our damned English 'ally'. Tostig had wormed his way into our ranks after he was exiled by the English the year before and I didn't like him. None of us did. He was an empty sort of a man – always out for a quick answer and always believing he was entitled to more than he was worth. He was a poor fighter, too – one of the first to fall, slain by his own people, the Saxons. A traitor's death; I felt no sorrow for him. Harald only took him on because of his knowledge of the land around York, though in the end that was sketchy at best. Perhaps, also, he took him on hoping that his brother would be as spoiled and useless as he, but that was not the case as his mad march north proved. Sadly for Harold, he would never march south again.

I think he'd hoped to surprise us and he might have done so had Harald not been thrown by Ulf's caution and sent spies far and wide. I can still see the messenger-lad's face as he spurred his horse toward us, the Saxon armies marching almost visibly across his dark pupils, just as men were setting down their shields and swords and scrambling for water from the river.

'The king,' he shouted. 'King Harold is come!'

The men might have panicked then, but Harald rose, caught the lad's bridle and looked him straight in the eye.

'No,' he said, his great voice echoing across the field, 'King Harald is already here!'

They cheered at that and cheered even louder when Harald told them how kind it was of the English to march so far north to save us the effort. And then, within moments, we were men no longer but a mass – an army. We found our shields and our places behind them with the ease of long practice. As Ulf had said, over and over, a good Viking is always ready for battle and were in place before the English were even close.

At first Harald sought to negotiate, to split England north and south as Cnut did with King Edmund at the start of his reign here, but the Saxon would have none of it – promised us no more land than seven of soil feet in which to bury our king. Harald admired that too, but declined the polite offer and raised his sword.

The Saxons fought hard. They near matched us for ferocity but we were fresher. We'd marched several long hours, yes, but they'd marched several long days. Even so, they might have had us if we had taken our armour off, so thank the Lord we did not – or, at least, thank Lord Ulf. Better sweat than blood.

We lost many all the same, including the Lord Ulf himself. He'd been very ill before we left Norway – a canker in his stomach that had looked like to fell him – but he had rallied, or so we'd thought. I think now that perhaps he was too weak all along and was simply determined to die on the battlefield like a true Viking, rather than wasting away in a bed like a woman.

I saw him go down. It is a picture frozen in my mind, so stark that it imprinted on the back of my eyes like a monk's illumination – except that no monk would paint that picture of horror. It was as if his knees collapsed beneath him, as if they'd endured one too many charges and could take no more. He staggered, tripped, righted himself but it was too late – he was isolated. The first I knew of the arrow in his throat was Harald's wail of desolation.

He bellowed like a speared bull, throwing his white blond head back to the sky in fury. But then, like the king he has always been, he took out his grief as he should – with the sword. I have heard men sing of warriors going berserker before but I thought it a bard's trick, an invention owing more to effect than truth. That day, though, I saw it for real. Harald ripped through the Saxons like an ancient fury, cutting a path right to the other Harold – and right through his heart too.

The Battle of Stamford Bridge did not last long after the eight-month king was dead. The Saxons turned and ran the minute Harold's standard fell and the field was ours – England was ours. Or so we thought. One thing only could spoil our victory, for no sooner had we installed ourselves in York than news came: Duke William had landed.

It was an annoyance, I'll tell you that. We'd scarce had time to set the boar over our new hearth-fire or to broach a second barrel of ale. The men had fought twice within the week and were not in the mood for more but we knew what must be done.

'Tis a gift really,' Harald said.

'A gift?' I asked him, incredulous.

'A gift,' he repeated, 'for now the English need us.'

He spoke true. A week later as we sailed our ships up the Thames we were ushered into Westminster as if they'd invited us there themselves. Edwin and Morcar sailed with us, having slunk out of hiding to prostrate themselves at Harald's feet. Morcar bent so low that when he rose again he had hound-dirt on his nose; we have called him Shitface ever since, though these days more in fondness than in derision.

The southern lords were every bit as eager to welcome us. The moment we came into view they wound up the great bridge that kept the royal palace safe from invaders, and they were all lining the banks of Westminster when we docked. Prince Edgar welcomed Harald on his knees and in return Harald presented him with Harold Godwinson's body – still intact and carried with respect. It is buried in the new abbey and monks say prayers over it every day in honour of a worthy adversary. Back then, though, it seemed that for the English one Harald was as good as another as long as he would wield a sword in their defence. But then, of course, wielding swords is what we Vikings do best.

The Normans had no chance. I'd heard tell that Duke William was a hardened warrior who'd defeated more rebellions in his own land than there are herring in a Spring catch, so why he trapped himself on a funny little peninsula in a funny little wooden castle I'll never know. It was almost laughable. I was in the lead ship with Harald as we rounded the coast and when we saw their fleet – if you can call it that – we thought perhaps it was a jest. The flagship was fine, newly built on a grand scale and gleaming with colour, but the rest were trade vessels or transport-boats, weighed down with wooden panelling to keep their precious horses safe. Ha! What use are horses against the Viking, save maybe seahorses?

Edwin and Morcar played their part. Eager to prove their worth to their new king and to keep their lands, they marched south with scores of Englishmen and joined battle with Duke William on the sloping land north of Hastings that we now call 'Victory Field'. Elizaveta oversaw the building of an abbey there afterwards, built in fine byzantine style and dedicated to our patron St Olaf, to celebrate the combined might of England and Norway seeing off the upstart southerners.

We made a good team. The English shield wall faced down the Norman cavalry and held against them for just the two short hours it took us to lead our Vikings up the road from the coast and right into their rear. They were decimated before the noontime meal and those that fled met only more Vikings lying in wait in our warships.

It was carnage. Scarce a woman in Normandy must have been left without a hole in her bed, though it didn't take us long to fill those! We took Normandy in 1067, Maine and Anjou in 1068, and France herself in 1070. After all that, Denmark had little choice but to surrender in 1071 and Harald was named as Emperor of a North far wider than even King Cnut controlled. It was a grand coronation the following year, with churchmen from all over Europe in attendance and both Harald and Elizaveta in empirical purple, as if Constantinople itself had come north, and the people cheering wildly and drinking the rich Norse ale Harald commanded fed into every fountain as the Romans used to do.

And they were right to cheer for he has been a fair ruler. I am biased, I know. My damned bed lies within the royal palace at Westminster so I am hardly like to criticise but it seems to me that, bar the usual gripes over taxes and harvests and law disputes that no earthly ruler could avoid, his subjects are content. Every land has its own regent, with power enough to rule as he wishes beneath Harald's overlordship, our shared coinage is stronger than any in the known world, and trade thrives. Who knows how it would have been if Harald had not succeeded, but in the face of such wealth, who cares? Personally, I consider myself privileged to have been a part of his journey all the way from those first vital victories at Fulford and Stamford Bridge. Privileged and proud.

Yes, 1066 was a fine year indeed and one I will gladly take to my grave as the year my dear King Harald Hardrada took the English throne and paved the way to becoming acclaimed ruler of this united Empire we all so proudly call our own – this English Empire.

AUTHOR'S NOTE

The biggest 'what if' of any 1066 discussion is 'what if Harold had beaten William at the Battle of Hastings' and, given that victory was only secured at the very end of the battle, it can safely be said to have been the closest call of all the events of that huge year. What is less regularly talked about, however – mainly because the battle was almost forgotten about in the near-instant demands of the next one – is 'What if Harold had *not* beaten Harald Hardrada at the Battle of Stamford Bridge.'

To be honest, if you'd been a betting man at the start of 1066, you would have probably put your hard-earned pennies on Hardrada. He'd won huge treasure as a mercenary all over Rus and Byzantine lands as a young man, then successfully taken Norway from his own nephew and held her in security and prosperity for twenty years before he challenged for England. He had an invasion force of thousands, sailing in three-hundred feared Viking warships, he came in alliance with Tostig who had been Earl of Northumbria for ten years before he was ousted in 1065, and he had some sort of backing from King Malcolm of Scotland. How did he ever lose?

Several things won King Harold the Battle of Stamford Bridge. One – perhaps the greatest one – was raw courage and determination. His miraculous march north from Westminster in the mere handful of days between Hardrada's huge victory at Fulford and the proposed hostage handover at Stamford Bridge, is truly the stuff of heroic poetry. The fact that they then caught the vicious Viking army by surprise, understrength and sunning themselves with their armour off, adds to the amazing tale of the victory. At the end of that battle King Harold must have truly felt that God was smiling upon him. Sadly, He wasn't!

What sort of a king would Hardrada have made? I'd

argue he'd have been a good one and certainly likely to be more culturally suited to ruling England than the Norman, William. Many Englishmen were still of Norse heritage, especially in the north and east, and it was not that long since Cnut had ruled – and ruled well. It is likely, I contend, that had Hardrada taken the English throne in 1066, he would have settled in with barely a ripple.

What's more, his wife – Elizaveta of Kiev (heroine of my novel *The Constant Queen*) – had sisters and brothers in the ruling houses of France, Hungary, Poland, Germany, Russia and even Byzantium. We would not, I believe, have been stuck as a 'northern backwater' with Harald and Elizaveta as our monarchs – but that, sadly, is not something we will ever know save in fiction.

Joanna Courtney
www.joannacourtney.com

DISCUSSION SUGGESTIONS

What might a Norse England have looked like, not just in the eleventh century but in the twelfth and thirteenth?

How much of our culture has come from our association with France in the medieval period?

APRIL
1066

*A*fter a largely successful tour of Northern England, including a grand coronation in York, King Harold and Queen Edyth headed back to Westminster to celebrate Easter in what must have been a cautiously optimistic mood. They had been cheered around the north and were rapturously welcomed back into Harold's heartlands in the south. Internally, for now at least, England was secure.

However, invasion forces were gathering in both Norway and Normandy. Spies would have reported the building of ships and massing of men, and it looked certain that there would be battle before the end of the fighting season.

And then, in the Easter skies, a strange 'dragon' or 'fire' tailed star was seen all over Europe – what we now know as Halley's Comet. In a time of great superstition and religious fervour this must have struck awe into the hearts of both common people and leaders. It was certainly seen as a sign from God. But a sign for whom? And signifying what...?

THE DRAGON-TAILED STAR
Carol McGrath

Harold Godwinson, as Earl of Essex and then Wessex, had taken
Edith Swanneck as a common-law wife. By her he had several
sons and daughters – all legitimate, for this was a legal marriage,
but not one blessed by the Church. Harold set his first wife aside,
however, when he became King, for he needed to confirm an
alliance with the earls of northern England, and the only way to
do so was to take their sister as wife.

It must have been hard for his sons and daughters by that first
wife to accept the second. Harder still for them to realise that he
was now vulnerable to outside threats and maybe even attempted
murder…

Thea stared up at the night sky wondering if King Edward
dwelled in Heaven, or was he one of the stars that glowed
through April's frosted darkness? She certainly never
considered Uncle Edward saintly. He had been stuffy and
pious – too devout, surrounding himself with Norman
priests, building a new abbey at Westminster, expecting
Aunt Edith to be kind and welcoming to his visitors from
across the Narrow Sea. Yet, Thea pondered, as she gathered
up her thirteen-year-old thoughts, in the end, Uncle
Edward *had* approved of her family and chosen her father,
Earl Harold, his brother by marriage, to rule the kingdom
after his death. It was a surprise to them all when the dying
king expressed his wishes as he had hovered between the
world of angels and a darker and very frightening place.
She shuddered and hurriedly crossed herself. Surely better
for Uncle Edward that he was a star in the night sky, than
facing the terrors that lay between Heaven and Hell?

Thea's father, King Harold, second of that name, had
been crowned on the day her Uncle Edward was interred
in his new abbey. Even though she was now a princess,
this was a mixed blessing. Her father had remarried,

taking Aldgyth, the sister of the powerful Northern earls and widow of a king of Wales, as his wife, claiming that marriage with Thea's mother, his true hand-fasted wife of eighteen years, was not approved by the Church. He told the family that since their union broke the Church rules on consanguinity – they were related at three times removed – he would have to marry the Northern widow to ensure her brothers' support and to keep the Church on his side.

'As you know well, there are too many greedy eyes on our kingdom. I must ally with her brothers if I am to protect England,' he had explained.

After his pronouncement, her father had sent her mother away. He had packed her, Thea, his elder daughter, off to Grandmother Gytha's household.

Thea stared up at the night sky, bright and star-dusted after several weeks of heavy cloud and cold rain, and wondered if she dared refuse to attend her father's Easter Court at Westminster. She could not be pleasant to the woman who had usurped her mother, though she still loved the huge, bearded warrior who was her father; a warrior who seemed to her as golden as the sun and gentle as the moon. She had another thought. Her childhood friend, Earl Waltheof, would join her father's Easter Court.

'You are coming and that is all there is to it, my girl. Sit up straight. It does not become a princess to be petulant.' Gytha peered closer at Thea's needlework. 'Just look at those stitches. You must improve your embroidery skills if you are to be a suitable wife for one of noble blood. Unpick that dragon.'

Tutting, Grandmother Gytha opened coffer after coffer, allowing their lids to crash down again. Finally, she found the box she wanted and dragged out the woollen blankets they might need for their journey. She called for maids to shake the fennel from them and repack them into a great leather travelling chest.

Thea said passionately, 'He married her, Grandmother. He married that woman whose brothers plagued him until he said yes. What about my mother? She should be my father's queen.'

'Do not speak of your stepmother in such a manner.' Gytha looked icily at her.

'I do not have a stepmother. I *have* a mother. That woman is a nithing to me.'

'You are ridiculous, girl. She is of our nobility, the queen, and your father is king. You cannot change what is. What is, is.'

'I refuse to bow to her.'

'You will bow to her, Thea. Now, leave your needlework. Go and ask Lady Agatha to help you pack your warmest clothing. The spring warmth has not yet arrived in England.' With those final words, Grandmother Gytha, the Countess of Wessex, stamped from the bower chamber, banging her eagle-headed walking stick against the coffers as she went.

Was it possible that Grandmother was angry at Harold's choice of bride, or was she just furious at her granddaughter's rebellious words? Wearily, Thea packed away her threads. She glared at the Wessex dragon stretched across her tapestry frame, a dragon still requiring much attention. For a moment, she fancied that the embroidered monster spat angrily at her too.

They rode from Heathfield on a misty April morning that promised to become a beautiful day once the sun reached its zenith and the light touch of early morning frost had disappeared. Thea, wearing a determined smile, mounted Lady, her grey palfrey, determined that today she would not antagonise the countess. Grandmother Gytha who, despite her sixty years, loved to ride, sat erect on her jennet, Juno, heavily booted feet set firmly in the stirrups below her divided riding gown and her voluminous mantle. The journey to London would take two days.

An hour after midday Grandmother announced that they would rest at the Bishop's Palace at St Albans. There, they could be assured of soft mattresses, linen sheets, and despite its being Lent, a delicious meal cooked by St Albans's excellent cook, Brother Lawrence, who had a talent with Lenten food, using spices and sauces in a clever way.

Thea glanced behind at the wagons carrying the maids, travelling chests and her grandmother's dismantled bed with its goose feather mattress which, once they reached Westminster, she must share. Thea sighed. At court, Grandmother would be watching her constantly. There would be no opportunity to seek the handsome Earl Waltheof and, once arrived, there would be a tapestry to finish during the month they would pass at the Easter Court. Grandmother never travelled to London without her embroidery threads. Under her sharp-eyed tutelage, the noble ladies would work on a hanging for the abbey building at Westminster, an Adam and Eve tapestry, begun at Christmastide and left aside once the court had dispersed.

Grandmother glared over at her as if she were reading her thoughts and Thea straightened up at once, reminded of how she must observe decorum. If she appeared contrite and obedient now, her grandmother might be lax in her vigilance and it might be possible to escape the palace bower halls to find her earl.

As they trotted through lanes ready to burst into leaf, along primrose-heavy banks and hedgerows threaded with robin-run-the-hedge, feeling the afternoon sun grow warmer on her back, Thea dreamed of her favourite dish – beef and mushrooms in a honeyed sauce – and imagined sharing the dish with the handsome blue-eyed young earl. She thought of the Eastertide festivities that would follow the feasting – the story telling, music and dancing long into the night. Smiling, content, she rode on.

When the cavalcade passed through the ancient Roman walls of St Albans, it was but a short trot to the Bishop's Palace hall. Sounds of activity echoed all around the abbey's palace courtyard: the stamping of horses, bridle bells jingling and usually silent monks noisily bustling here and there. Although the countess had expected them to be the only visitors, the abbey was as hectic as a market day in a town.

'What is occurring here?' The countess leaned down over Juno's proud head to speak to the gatekeeper.

'The king's train has arrived. He is on the way to the Easter Court at Westminster.'

Bishop Erwald, seeing their arrival, hurried across the yard. 'Welcome, Countess! We are to have great company this night…so honoured. Come, come, and dismount. Brother Hubert will escort you and the princess to your chamber. Not the best chamber, I fear, but I promise it is the second best.'

Gytha snorted as a groom helped her down from Juno. 'Make sure it is warmed with a brazier and that there is a chamber close by for my maids.'

'Of course, Lady Countess. All is ready, just as your messengers requested,' he purred, his bishop's cloak sweeping low about his portly figure as he bowed.

Gytha said, 'It is right that the best chamber should be made ready for the king, my son. Make sure it is aired and has every comfort for him and his queen.'

The bishop replied graciously, 'Of course, nothing has been spared, Countess.' He bowed low again.

His obsequious manner irritated Thea. He was

compensating for the fact that his mother had been foreign, Norman, and that these days the tide favoured all that was truly English. Refusing the groom's help, she slid down effortlessly from her palfrey. A stable boy raced forward, removed her valuable jewel-studded saddle and gave it into the keeping of Gytha's servants. The groom led both horses away.

Countess Gytha leaned on her stick and, ignoring the bishop, testily commanded, 'Lead on, Brother Hubert.'

An hour later, their grimed travel garb exchanged for more suitable indoor attire, Thea was sorting out Gytha's embroidery threads. A clatter of horses' hooves passed through the gates and into the courtyard that lay below the chamber and she flew to the window to push back the shutters. Lady Margaret, the Countess's senior lady, and their little maid Grete, followed her and they all peered down at the elegantly clad cavalcade that was pouring through the abbey gates and into the yard.

'My father, oh, and Uncle Leofwine is there too!' Thea called over her shoulder to the countess. Added, with less enthusiasm, 'And Lady Aldgyth.'

'Queen Aldgyth,' Lady Margaret reprimanded, pointing to the gleaming gold-and-jewelled coronet that secured Lady Aldgyth's fluttering silk veil in place.

Thea snapped a retort. 'Never a queen. Only my mother is *his* queen.'

Gytha rose from her place beside the brazier and, using her eagle-headed stick, tapped her way to the window. 'Do not say that to your father, my girl. You will guard your tongue. Remember, you cannot change what is. Fetch me my cloak, Margaret, I'll greet them both.'

'How could he marry that woman?' Thea cried with angry passion. Before her grandmother could answer, she snatched up her cloak, flew from the chamber and hurried down the wooden stairs into the yard to greet her father; all efforts at decorum forgotten. Once she had pushed her way through the crowd of retainers and past the fawning Bishop Erwald, she ignored the lady standing by her father's side and threw herself at him. 'Father!' she exclaimed, 'you are here.'

'Thea! So *you* are here too – how well met! Where is your grandmother?'

'She is coming, Father.'

Harold glanced at the lady by his side, a woman who was no longer a plain-clad noble widow but regally dressed in rich ruby colours, her sleeves embroidered with tiny gold dragons. 'My daughter, Theodora Gytha,' he said.

'I know who she is,' the woman said quietly, 'but, should a royal daughter be greeting her father before such a great company as if she were a common serving girl?'

Thea drew back. She clenched her fists by her side. 'My lady, I am not common nor a servant. I do, however love and cherish my father and I wish to speak with him. Alone.'

'Come now, Thea, at dinner we shall have much conversation. Your stepmother is correct, you must behave like a princess. Look, here comes your grandmother now! I must greet her, and then my wife and I will rest a while.'

Feeling her cheeks redden to the colour of her hair at the reprimand, Thea bowed her head and backed away into the gathered crowd. No one noticed her, everyone was too busy fussing around her father and his new wife – Thea could not bear to name her as queen; after all, she was not anointed and crowned as Aunt Edith had been when she had married Uncle Edward. She watched as her father was ushered by the bishop and her grandmother towards the apartments appointed for him and his retinue. She heard the bishop's fawning voice say, 'My lord, may we send refreshments? The next meal will not be served for a while yet.'

· · ·

Thea was certain that she saw a blond-headed young thane following the royal party withindoors, but he had not seen her. Petulant, she glanced at the great candle clock that burned time away by the main hall's entrance, then, instead of returning to their chamber she hurried to the kitchen buildings that stood apart from all the other wooden buildings in case of the spread of fire.

A servant ran past her and banged with his fist on the kitchen door. The cook came to the doorway. He was not the usual burly, red-faced and kindly Brother Lawrence Thea had known from previous visits. This cook was tall and thin with his hair cropped short at the back of his neck in Norman fashion.

The servant spoke breathlessly. 'The king would like a dish of spiced pears in wine, and a plate of wafers. Meantime, a jug of hippocras and two cups, if you please.'

The cook peered out of the doorway past the boy, glancing around the still bustling courtyard, almost as if he were looking for someone. Thea slipped out of sight behind a pile of empty wine barrels. Disappearing inside the cook reappeared a moment later with a jug and two cups as requested.

'Take this to our Lord King,' he stated, 'return for the pears.'

Thea waited until the servant had scurried off. Stepping out from her hiding place she brazenly banged on the kitchen door. The same cook appeared.

'I am Theodora Gytha, the king's daughter. Where is Master Lawrence? I wish to speak with him.'

The cook looked her up and down as if he did not believe her. 'He does not work here now. He has been transferred to St Benet's.' The new cook had a slight accent Thea could not quite place.

'That is the monastery my mother endows,' she

remarked and added, 'I was looking forward to his honeycakes.' Not waiting for a reply, she added, 'Well, I am visiting my mare. I want a treat for her.' She did not wait to be invited in, but pushed her way past the thin man who stood gaping at her, his eyes hooded and unrevealing. She marched through the kitchen ignoring the servants who were preparing vegetables, salads, and broiling fish in a copper pan over the open fire. The scent of herbs and poaching pears wafted a delicious fragrance that rose in a steaming curl from a pot on a brazier. Thea looked about her, not recognising any of the kitchen servants. Moreover, they all wore their hair in the Norman manner, cut short at the back. She hurried over to a tray of fresh-made bread and seizing a small loaf, sped back to the open door, where the new cook glared at her as she pushed past.

'Surely you have servants to fetch and carry for you?' he called after her.

'I prefer to care for Lady myself,' she retorted.

Thea found a suitable saddle and bridle and harnessed Lady as the horse contentedly munched hay. Thankful that the stable boys were too busy with the king's horses to notice her, Thea led the mare from the stables, mounted, and arranging her woollen gown so that it fell with some modesty over her legs, she trotted past a few more riders entering through the abbey gateway, her hood drawn close about her face.

'Keep to the side! Allow way for King Harold's thanes!' someone called after her.

Thea raised an arm in acknowledgement, then patting Lady's neck she trotted out of the gates and, kicking into a canter, went along the Roman road until she discovered a pathway that led into the woods. She was pleased to be amongst trees without attendants, spring sunshine caressing her back, and bird song all around. No one cared about her and, after all, who would miss her for an hour or two? Grandmother Gytha would be with the king and his wife. She was a traitor, not only to Thea and her sister, packed off to Wilton Abbey for her education, but to her brothers who had been sent to the Irish court, and to her mother, the most beautiful of all mothers, Elditha of the long swan-like neck. Thinking mutinous thoughts, Thea cantered on through the woods, avoiding overhanging branches, quieting her thoughts with the scent of fresh grass, primroses, and dandelions clustered over banks and alongside ditches. Slowing to a walk, she glimpsed a pale blue spring sky, decorated with small clouds that drifted above the new-budded beech trees like puffs of white smoke. She met no one else as she rode along the winding deer tracks, but coming to a fast-flowing river, she realised that the shadows had lengthened and there was now a chill in the air, making the wood feel less friendly. She turned Lady around and following her mare's hoof prints, headed back to the bishop's grand palace.

As Thea trotted through the abbey gates the Vespers bell was ringing. If she hurried she could still attend the service. Handing Lady to a stable boy, giving sharp orders to rub her down and not to feed her too many oats, she made her way up wooden stairs to the chamber she was to share with her grandmother. She would clean her dusty boots, change her stockings and throw on her best cloak. Her gown smelt a little of horse sweat, but no one would notice. Grandmother would already be seated at the front of the abbey church. Thea planned to slip in quietly and pretend that she had been with Lady in the stables, or maybe she could say she had fallen asleep in one of the side chapels? It would only be half a lie, and after all, did it matter whether the peace of the woods, or prayer to Our Lady had quietened her unsettling anger?

Grandmother, however, was not at Vespers. She stood erect in the middle of the chamber, her face the colour of bleached linen. The countesses' maids, equally pale-faced and weeping gathered around her. Gytha stamped her stick into the floor rushes, scattering camomile and wisps of straw. 'Where have you been, child? Gadding about the abbey gardens, no doubt, wasting your time in idleness as your father lies ill in his chamber.'

Thea swallowed. How could this be? She had seen him only a few hours ago and had felt his strong embrace. Before she could speak, her Grandmother seized her by her arms and shook her. 'You must learn to curb this wilful disobedience, child, or no man shall want you as wife, even if your father is the king. Even if he does survive this dreadful illness which has overcome him!' Gytha took several breaths to calm herself, grasped Thea's wrist. 'You had better come with me.' She turned to Lady Margaret. 'Go with my ladies to church, say that I am resting. Pray for my son's recovery but tell no one that he is unwell.'

Lady Margaret inclined her head and, turning to the flock of women, said, 'Dry your eyes. Fetch your mantles.'

When Thea saw her father lying on a couch, his breath rasping, sweat beaded on his brow, his countenance pale, with Bishop Erwald by his side and Lady Aldgyth seated at his feet, she thought of how Aunt Edith had prayed at Uncle Edward's feet during his final hours at Christmastide. She remembered the atmosphere in the palace the night that her father was chosen by England's noblemen to be king. How odd that now her father might be dying and her stepmother sat warming his cold feet in her lap. Her father opened his eyes and seeing her, weakly beckoned her to his side. She leaned closer to catch his words.

'Your mother,' he whispered, 'if I die, tell her I have

always loved her. If I die this night, Godwin must return from Ireland to take my place.'

As her father sank back onto his pillow, Thea looked from her father to his wife, to Bishop Erwald, and from him to her grandmother. 'He thinks he will die. He wants Godwin home. What has happened?' Her voice broke, choked with tears.

'We do not know,' Bishop Erwald said. 'He has difficulty breathing. We have sent for the apothecary, and the king's brother.'

Gytha sat wearily at a table, pushing dirty dishes aside. Frowning, she sniffed at one, at a small slice of pear left uneaten. 'Almonds,' she said sharply with a flash of understanding. 'Were almonds in the sauce? They are poison to him. The cooks know it. You know it, Bishop.' She pointed again to the empty dish on the table.

Aldgyth glanced up. 'I was unaware of this malignant thing with almonds!'

'You should have been told,' Gytha snapped, 'though Brother Lawrence knows that almonds can harm my son.'

'There is a new cook here,' Thea declared. 'All within the kitchens are different from when last we were here. I saw them when I went to fetch a treat for Lady.'

Gytha frowned at the bishop. 'Is this so?'

Bishop Erwald paled and began to stutter. 'We, we were sent a new cook just recently, from Bishop Lanfranc's employ. He has served in Rome; has prepared dishes for the Pope himself. It was an honour to receive him and his servants. Brother Lawrence has gone to St Benet's.'

Thea was confused. She studied Bishop Erwald's countenance. Why had he employed a cook who had been in Lanfranc's employ? Lanfranc was a known Norman supporter. He had the ear and the trust of Duke William himself.

Her grandmother must have harboured the same thoughts, for she rose abruptly to her feet and swept the used dishes to the floor. 'A cook in Lanfranc's employ? Madness! Treachery!'

Bishop Erwald stammered, 'The...the apothecary will be here soon...'

As he spoke, Brother Simon, the abbey's apothecary, swept into the chamber, with Harold's brother, Leofwine, close at heel. Attention shifted hopefully to the little monk as he hurried to the king's side. Countess Gytha explained about the almonds.

'We must make him vomit,' the monk said after smelling Harold's breath and listening to his breathing. 'We must purge his body thoroughly.' Within moments he had given the king salt water to drink, lifted him and held a receptacle for him to vomit into.

Aldgyth rose and peered into the bowl. 'It is not enough.' She turned to the apothecary. 'If you have powder of the honeybee, that might work. My first husband required it for one of his children by a mistress. Soak it on a sponge with vinegar and make him suck on the mixture.'

'We can try. Send for my assistant to fetch what is needed from my herbal, Bishop.'

The bishop, clearly annoyed at being so ordered, but also embarrassed by his cook's innocent mistake – if indeed it was innocent – hastened out of the chamber, calling for someone to fetch Brother Simon's assistant. With nothing he could do to help, Leofwine also took his leave. 'We must ensure calm is kept,' he said through gritted teeth. 'This has been a poor day's work done here.'

Thea watched as the monk and Aldgyth together assisted her father to vomit again, and again. Exhausted, he lay back, shivering despite the chamber's great warmth.

'What will happen to the crown if he dies?' Gytha murmured. 'The hornets will swarm again.'

'We must send for Godwin. That is my father's wish,' Thea announced firmly.

The countess looked tired, and old. 'The Witan may

choose another earl since Godwin is not yet a warrior. And, he is in Ireland.'

'Then, send for him. A dying king's wish must not be ignored.'

'He is not yet dying,' Brother Simon said with firmness. 'I will bleed him to reduce the fever. There is no need to send for his son.'

Aldgyth raised her hand imperiously. 'Bleeding will weaken him. Wait until we see if the honeybee purgative works.'

Harold's breathing was becoming more laboured and shallow. He was shivering, his limbs as cold as ice, but his flesh was sweating as they piled furs and covers around him. Thea sat quiet to one side in fervent prayer, and Gytha pursing her lips, complained that the bishop must be in the orchard collecting bees to powder, he was so long in returning.

'Or announcing that Harold is in mortal danger,' snapped Aldgyth, as she wiped her groaning husband's brow and held his cold hand.

The king was hovering between the world of the living and the dead, Brother Simon opened his satchel to fetch out his knife and bleeding cups. Breathless, the bishop hurried through the door, ushering Brother Simon's assistant before him. 'We could not find the powdered honeybee,' the boy explained, anxious, 'I discovered it in the wrong place.'

'Here,' the bishop added, giving items to Brother Simon. 'Vinegar and a sponge.'

'Small sips only for now,' Aldgyth said, as Brother Simon handed her the mixed potion, clearly intending to administer the concoction to her husband herself. 'And more later, when two notches of the candle have burned down.' She tossed Bishop Erwald a stony-hard glance. 'I shall care for the king myself, with my lord's mother and

68

daughter and Brother Simon. You are not required, go, attend your duties. And take away those other things which you brought with you. They, also, are not needed.' She indicated a silver bowl of holy water and the last rights requisites that belonged to death's ritual.

Thea was impressed at how her stepmother had taken efficient control. She knelt where Lady Aldgyth had sat by her father's feet and prayed silently to Theodora, her name-day saint. *If Lady Aldgyth can save my father's life, I shall never complain about her ever again.*

Countess Gytha held her son's hand as Aldgyth and the apothecary helped Harold to vomit again. Aldgyth lifted his head, stroked back his damp hair and wiped his forehead with a damp cloth. She calmly, but insistently, encouraged him to live. Into the quiet of the night the three women sat by the king's side until, at last, his breathing eased. Compline and the hour of nine had passed, with the abbey's sconces lit in the courtyard and corridors, his fever broke. Harold drifted into sleep, and the crisis was over.

The bishop returned an hour before Matins, his relief at the king's comfort evident.

'I want all dishes served from henceforth tasted by one of my lord's men,' Gytha ordered, ignoring the bishop's apparent relief.

'I fear your order comes too late,' a voice said from the doorway. Thea's uncle, Leofwine, stepped from the shadows. 'I personally ensured the self-same request, but there was no deliberate poison intended, bar that for one victim alone.'

He strode further into the room, bowed to the queen, but addressed his mother. 'We discovered the cook leaving via the herb garden gate. His attempt on my brother's life was deliberate but we cannot prove it. He claims he knew nothing about almonds.' Leofwine looked accusingly at the half-Norman bishop who shook his head in innocence. 'He knew nothing, yet the abbey knows of the king's abhorrence of them. You know of this fact.' Leofwine smiled maliciously. 'No matter. Your traitorous cook is safely secured in a monk's cell.'

Bishop Erwald seemed unruffled. 'He will be returned to Italy in disgrace. He will face justice in Rome.' He gave a cursory bow and swept from the chamber.

'No, he will not escape that way,' Leofwine said, as with his mantle flowing behind him he hurried after the bishop. 'He will be boiled alive in a sauce of his choosing and you, my lord Bishop, will never be trusted again.' Leofwine's raging continued until the three women heard the outer door slam with a heavy thud.

'There will be no proof of guilt, or of the bishop's involvement in all this,' Gytha said, 'but, I vow, if Erwald has turned to support Normandy – and has sanctioned attempted murder, he will pay. There are ways to deal with treacherous monks.'

Aldgyth raised her eyebrows and looked over at Thea. When she smiled, Thea found herself returning the smile. Grandmother Gytha could be trusted to guard her son's interests and Bishop Erwald would not escape her wrath. Yet, whilst close to death, her father had whispered comforting words to her and she knew that in his heart he still loved her mother.

Excusing herself, she wandered from the stuffy, foul-smelling chamber into the abbey cloisters in search of sweeter air. Although her beloved father was safely delivered from a terrible fate, what would happen if he died? Would the Witan ever accept her brother as father's successor?

The night sky was lit up with stars. A group of monks stood, staring up at a bright new star that had appeared as if summoned by a sorcerer. Some were praying, others were pointing as they clutched each other's robes. Through the gaps in the pillars, Thea watched some of her father's attendants also gathering – was that Earl Waltheof amongst them? She shook her head, no, her thoughts were no longer for him. Rather, they had settled firmly upon the importance of her father's survival and his kingdom. She looked into the sky to the enormous star with a dragon-like tail hovering above the abbey church.

Uncle Leofwine stepped beside her. 'They say such a long-tailed star indicates great change in a kingdom. Let us hope it means that your father is to be promised a long and peaceful reign.'

'Amen,' Thea said softly. 'May God protect all of us – my father, his queen and our people from the evil that lies across the Narrow Sea.'

'And from the treachery of Norman-loving bishops,' Leofwine said with not a little hint of cynicism.

AUTHOR'S NOTE

This story takes place in April 1066 after Harold has set aside his common law wife of nearly two decades who had six living children with him by 1066, two girls and four boys. How did his elder daughter feel when her father married a Northern noblewoman to gain support from her brothers, the Northern earls?

I wondered what might have happened had Harold died before the Norman Conquest in October. It also seems obvious that the Normans had sympathisers and spies in England prior to the Conquest – just as Harold had spies in Normandy.

The Comet (now called Halley's Comet) is depicted in the Bayeux Tapestry, which doesn't rank as a scientific paper, but we know a lot about the 'star' from astronomers in the Far East. For the Chinese, the sky was the mirror of the Earth, so any danger to the Emperor would be revealed in the heavens.

Their records state:

'In the third year of Ch'ih Ping, in the third month, on the

day Ki Wei [2 April 1066], a broom star whose tail was about seven cubits appeared in the east sky in Pisces in the morning.' After passing the Sun: 'On the Koei Wei [26 April] the broom star appeared with the vapour like a pint of flour... After 67 days the star and the vapour all disappeared.'

The Anglo-Saxon Chronicle states:
'At that time, throughout all England, a portent such as men had never seen before was seen in the heavens... It first appeared on the eve of the festival of Letania Maior, that is on 24 April, and shone every night for a week.' This introduces an interesting debate. The comet would have appeared, its tail streaming one way, vanished as it passed the sun, then reappeared, its tail spreading in the opposite direction.

Why has the ASC only mentioned it the once, as it left our Solar System, not when it first appeared? There is probably a very simple answer for early April...

The English weather!

Carol McGrath
www.carolcmcgrath.co.uk

DISCUSSION SUGGESTIONS

What must it have been like to fall ill in the 11th century – or at any time before the introduction and understanding of modern medicine?

What was childhood like in the past? Did girls, and boys, have a chance to play?

What sort of games or toys would they have enjoyed?

MAY / JUNE
1066

*F*or the ordinary people across England, summer 1066 must have unrolled as usual, but for those in charge things were starting to escalate – especially in the seas around her southern and eastern coasts.

Tostig Godwinson harried the English coastline with a small fleet of ships launched from his father-in-law's country of Flanders, sailing via the Isle of Wight up the southern coast before being seen off by Earls Edwin and Morcar and fleeing to Scotland to await his Viking ally.

It was enough, though, for King Harold to call out the 'fyrd' – the general army raised from service owed to the crown by a certain number of men in every town and village across the country. They were stationed on the south coast as clearly it was felt that the threat from Normandy was, if not greater than Norway, at least more immediate.

They were in for a long wait...

IF YOU CHANGED ONE THING

Richard Dee

What if someone, one day in the future invented a time machine and was able to go back in time? That person would need to be very careful because just one, small, thing could alter the history of big things…

I liked to ask my senior class a question on a Friday, it was the end of the week and their concentration on work was fading with the prospect of two days off. History had to be made interesting, at least I had always thought so and I tried to make Fridays a bit different. We had been going through important events and had been discussing how small changes might have had big effects. The trivial things that would change everything, a lame horse, a shower of rain, someone who had lived or died differently.

They were a lively group and we ranged through the ages asking 'what if'? There was the usual frustration in the lack of good evidence for a lot of history and someone remarked that history would be so much better if we had a time machine and we could just go and have a look for ourselves. All the usual things, we could see if Jesus was real, maybe stop the slaughter of the First World War, or find out what really happened to the dinosaurs were the favourites.

These were all good ideas but not my personal choice; I wanted to see if it was true about the Battle of Hastings. After all, in six months it would be the millennium of the event and it was in the public eye, the last time in our history that foreign troops had been on our soil in any numbers. A few had made it into Wales in 1797 but as far as I was concerned that didn't count. And the outcome at Hastings, at least according to what we knew, rested on a sequence of small events and a trick. This particular Friday I raised the subject, handing out printed sheets with the historical facts as we knew them.

We discussed the accounts, William of Poitiers, William of Malmesbury and the Anglo-Saxon Chronicles. Each gave differing stories and we debated them. There was so much conflicting information that it was hard to summarise the events that really mattered. In the end, we agreed that the disbanding of the army on the south coast was the first step.

'OK prof,' said Martin, the most opinionated of the group, 'This looks like another job for your theoretical time machine.'

I nodded my agreement. Martin continued, 'If you could go back, what would you do?'

'Any ideas?' I threw the debate open to the class.

'You could leave the standing army on the coast?' and, 'Split your force and send some north to Stamford?' were a couple of the more sensible suggestions along with, 'Send an expedition to France and destroy the ships.'

'Not bad,' I said, 'but let's think back to the comet, Harold took it as a bad omen, maybe you could convince him it was a good one.'

'How?' asked one of the girls, I decided to throw my curve ball into the debate.

'I'd go to Winchester,' I said, 'to Harold's court; before the invasion, I'd warn Harold of the danger from William and from the Scandinavians.'

'Why?' said Lydia, 'surely that would change everything. If the army stays then they would not go to Stamford Bridge, maybe the Norse invasion succeeds and who knows what happens, we would be a different country, we might not even exist.'

There was laughter from the group. Some of them suggested that they could think of a few teachers who wouldn't be missed, I was pleased that my name wasn't among them.

'And this is the problem,' I said. 'If you change one thing then it changes everything.'

'But what about the weight of events?' asked Laura, 'surely one little thing might change a few details but the effect would be local, there must be a collective inertia to major upheaval.'

'You're right, Prof,' said Bryan, 'you must be careful not to change anything.' He stopped talking as the class realised what he had said and turned to look at him.

Bryan, one of the quiet ones, there's always one at the back, the girls ignored him, he was safe and therefore boring, they hung out with the risky lads, the loud and the brash attracted them but I could see that Bryan could change the world. He was a brilliant student and his work was insightful and well researched. A little over dramatic occasionally and sometimes he wrote as if he was remembering instead of describing, but that was just his way of expressing himself.

'Sounds like you're an expert Bryan,' said Greg, the class loudmouth, and Bryan coloured and slouched lower in his seat.

'I meant that you would have to be careful,' he muttered but by then everyone else was shouting about butterfly effects and the movie, how hot Ashton Kutcher had been and suddenly we were on to killing your grandfather.

'Quiet,' I shouted as it started to get out of hand. 'Whatever Bryan said we all know what he means. Logically we can't travel in time because of the paradoxes that time travel creates. No matter how we tried we would rewrite history, even killing an insect or saying hello to a man in the street might have consequences we couldn't predict. We can theorise about how much things would change but we don't really know. For the sake of this discussion let's pretend. I said I'd warn Harold, how could I do it?'

'Dress it up as prophecy, maybe as a monk travelling from the east who has had a vision.' Helen, one of the girls and Greg's number one fan, spoke up.

'It would be too risky to tell him,' I countered, 'you might be thought of as a sorcerer, Harold could have you killed.'

'They were a superstitious lot back then, it might be better to arrive on the battlefield and warn him there.' This suggestion was from David, Greg's foil.

Jayne was not so sure, 'Of course, the trouble is that if you managed to warn him, and save him, what would happen to your time? Would you even be able to come back if the conditions that let you build the time machine never existed?'

Now we were getting into the paradox situation again. Everyone started shouting, drowned out by Greg, dripping with sarcasm, 'Well Prof, I guess we'll never know, cos no one's ever built one.'

The bell sounded for the end of the day and before the scramble to leave I shouted, 'For Monday; I want all of you to read the notes, think of a single moment in the event. Tell me about how it affects the whole story and how, if it changed, it would change the whole outcome, tell me all about it.'

'Can I have a word?' Bryan, as the class filed out into the corridor, hung back. His face was screwed up as if he was struggling with his conscience and I wondered why.

'Can I tell you something in confidence?' he said.

I sat on a wooden desk, 'Of course you can.'

'I'm going to do it,' he told me.

'Do what, Bryan?'

'Go back like you said and have a look, I can come back and tell you on Monday.'

He said it in a matter of fact tone as if it was a perfectly natural thing to do. 'But Bryan, that would mean…'

He nodded, 'That's right Prof.'

'You mean there is a real time machine and you've used it?'

'Oh yes,' he said, 'a simple one, it's my father's

invention really, he works for the government as you know, well they've been developing one and they've got it working. It's supposed to be a secret but I know where it is. On Sundays I can get into where they keep it. I've done it several times and not been noticed.'

I was staggered. I knew that Bryan's father was a scientist but it all sounded a bit too improbable. I decided to play along.

'So where have you been?'

'All the places you've talked about on Fridays, I've seen them all.'

'Have you any proof?'

He was different now, animated and enthusiastic, an expert sharing his knowledge.

'Well, you can't take anything in case you drop it. Imagine if archaeologists found a phone that was hundreds of years old. You wear the control on your wrist like a watch. You only stop for a few minutes and it pulls you back automatically. The vital thing you mustn't do is leave a trace or change anything so you have to be really careful.'

It sounded to me like he had thought about telling me this, there were so many questions I wanted to ask but Bryan was still talking.

'I try and keep in the distance, the machine isn't that accurate anyway, so I try and arrive miles away from the action but at least that way I'm not noticed. All my clothes and everything have to be right as well, you can't stand out. They're a suspicious lot in the past, everyone's a witch or everything is an omen. But I will go and I'll tell you what I find.'

There was more, he looked over my shoulder and wouldn't meet my gaze. 'What else is there Bryan?'

'Nothing,' he mumbled, 'I have to go.'

I stood between him and the door. 'Bryan, I know there's more, just tell me, I can help you.'

He swallowed, wrestling with his conscience, 'You won't believe me, you can't, nobody does.'

'What do you mean?' He wasn't making any sense.

'It sounds so stupid and there's no proof, but I think I have changed something already. You know our house?'

It was a grand one on the seafront, in a row all painted in pastel colours. Bryan's was palest blue. 'Yes,' I nodded, 'it's the blue one.'

'No!' it was an anguished cry, 'when I went last time I remember our house was yellow. When I came back it was blue. I'm the only one who remembers.' He pushed past me and ran down the rather revolting lime green corridor, his footsteps echoing on the tiles.

I spent all weekend in a panic, had Bryan gone? Could he go? Perhaps he was messing me around, playing a trick on me? Maybe he was delusional. I felt tense, expecting to see everything change around me as it all went wrong. In the end everything was quiet, I spent the time marking work, had leisurely meals on my own, and a Sunday afternoon stroll along the cliff path and seafront. It was irrational of course. Thinking logically about it, Bryan had said he had gone to lots of places and we were all still here, life was carrying on as normal as far as we could tell. The paint colour had to be a mistake, I saw it at least once a week and it had always been pink.

Sunday night I couldn't sleep, in the end I got up and paced, willing the hours to pass. And I got angry, angry with Bryan for leading me on, angry with myself for letting a student sucker me. I turned the conversation over and over in my head until finally at four a.m., I slept.

I got up again at seven and prepared for another day. I had the history class after the first break and now felt that the joke was on me. Nothing had changed in the world. There were still wars; destruction and the same old political squabbles dominated the news. In a way it felt so comforting.

The school building was the same red brick, the blue corridors and white plastic desks, just like they always had been.

Bryan was first in after the whistle. 'I've been,' he said. He was subdued, his face lined with worry.

'What happened, why do you look so frightened? You changed nothing, look we're all still here, everything is normal.'

His face was a terrible sight, 'You don't remember do you?' he asked.

'Don't remember what? Bryan, you'll have to explain.'

He took a deep breath, 'All right, I went back on Sunday morning, I used the machine and found myself in some woods. I could hear the sounds of a battle quite close, shouts and clanging. There was a whistling in the air, arrows I guess, and I crept closer for a better look. The grass was damp, it was a cold day.'

'Go on.' This was amazing, either the product of an overactive imagination, or a real experience.

'I could see over a crest, I think I was near a ditch because there was a terrible stench, sort of like rusty iron and a lot of moaning. Then I realised that it came from a heap of bodies, just lying there like a pile of rubbish. There was the odd limb twitching. Flies everywhere. I'd never seen anything like it before and I was sick, really sick.'

I wasn't surprised, and at that moment I believed him, his account was too vivid, the closest any of us got to the horror of hand-to-hand warfare was reading about it. He must be telling the truth. And blood smelt of iron.

'I was distracted and the next thing I knew I had been grabbed by two soldiers. I thought I was done for, that I was going to die a thousand years before I was born. I couldn't look at my wrist to see how long I had before I came back. I couldn't understand a word they said, but they dragged me up to a hilltop where there was a group around a large banner. I knew that it was Harold and that I was in big trouble.'

Just then Greg and his mates sauntered in and Bryan slunk away to his place at the back. I needed to know the rest, how had he got away and returned without changing anything? The class were all assembled; I put my thoughts to the back of my mind and got on with the lesson.

'Right then, on Friday we were discussing what single event would have changed everything and given us a different outcome.' There was silence, I thought that Bryan might speak up, but he remained silent.

'Anyone want to start?' I asked. No one answered, they were quieter than usual. No one wanted to be first.

I went round the class, picking people at random, I deliberately left Bryan out, I wanted to keep him to the end. The other students gave various trite answers; the weather, William's feint retreat and the presence of the track between the hills.

Greg spoke up; he liked the sound of his own voice. Outwardly he pretended not to care, mainly to impress the ladies. But under it all he had a fine mind. 'I think it's here,' he said, pointing to one of the printed sheets I had given them all, 'in the account of William of Malmesbury.'

'That's the least reliable one, Greg,' I said, 'it was written well after the event.'

'Yes sir, but I looked at it again this morning and saw what I hadn't noticed before.' He waved the paper and everyone else rustled their work as they looked for their copies.

'Well, Greg?' I gave him a minute, 'Do enlighten us.'

'It's all here sir; in William's account, this is the moment that it all might have changed.'

He read aloud; *'And in the midst of Harold's group they brought to him a stranger, dressed as a monk and speaking a foreign tongue. His men found him wandering behind the lines, and fearing he was an agent of the Duke, had captured him. They now presented him for judgement. The stranger called out to Harold in his own tongue, Harold turned his head to gaze upon him, and an arrow hit his helmet's cheek-piece and bounced away with a spark. Had the King not turned at that instant the arrow would surely have transfixed his eye and done him much harm. There was disorder around the banner, and more so when the stranger was no longer to be found.'*

'That's it,' Greg said, 'the stranger saved Harold, if he had been a second later then our Angleland would have had a very different future.'

'And King Aethal would not be able to trace his line back to Harold,' broke in Greta, 'the longest unbroken royal house in Europa. Hell, we might even have been ruled by *le Francois!*'

I looked at Bryan; he sat in the corner as ever, I rarely noticed him. He looked at me and said nothing, but his eyes were full of tears. He was shaking his head as if the weight of the whole world was on him. I didn't understand why, perhaps he would tell me later. After all; I still had to hear how he had escaped without changing history.

'Who do you think the stranger was?' I said to the class, 'I suppose we'll never know.'

'Unless we had a time machine,' said Greg.

AUTHOR'S NOTE

I've tried to bring a science fiction twist to the history, perhaps something that you might not expect. The minute events that taken together shape the flow of human experience has always fascinated me, and I'm forever wondering 'what if'? Here I have tried to project that into a story. What if you could go back and change things, even if you hadn't meant to would it be impossible not to? And what would be the result?

My particular passion is writing science fiction with an

emphasis on the realistic. I believe in putting familiar things and situations in a different setting rather than reinventing everything.

Richard Dee
www.richarddeescifi.co.uk

DISCUSSION SUGGESTIONS

If you had a time machine, what one event in history would you want to change and why?

If you could travel back in time, how could you ensure the 'Butterfly Effect' would not occur (the theory that even to inadvertently kill one butterfly in the past, the present – the future – would be dramatically changed)?

JULY

1066

*I*n Normandy the single biggest concern for William and his lords was the critical problem of how to get their horses over the Narrow Sea (the English Channel). Normans fought on horseback – that is to say, Norman nobles fought on horseback. William also had a vast infantry force and a significant number of crossbowmen, but the intimidation of a Norman army was in its mounted cavalry. To go into battle without them was unthinkable but the Normans were used to fighting in northern France where they could ride to meet their enemies.

Despite their long coastline, Normandy had no navy so the Narrow Sea was a huge barrier. The only expertise they had to draw on were those men who had returned from the less well known but equally impressive Norman Conquest of Italy and Sicily in the years leading up to 1066. Under their guidance, much effort was put into the building of a fleet of vessels to transport not just the men but the horses to England to invade.

The 'Ship List' is one of our few primary sources for the crucial year of 1066. It lists all the major Norman lords and the number of ships they provided for William, and is a fascinating testament to the scale of the operation. Some ships would have been commandeered from traders, or bought in from other, more seafaring nations but many were built for this one purpose – to invade England...

A ROMAN INTERVENES
Alison Morton

Roma Nova is an imaginary country, a remnant of the Western Roman Empire. Founded (in the author's imagination) in AD 395 by dissident pagans when Theodosius enforced Christianity throughout the Empire, the tiny mountain state has negotiated or fought its way through the unstable, dangerous times of the Roman dusk and the Early Middle Ages.

Daughters as well as sons carried weapons to defend their homeland, their gods and their way of life. Fighting danger side-by-side with brothers and fathers on equal terms reinforced women's status and enhanced their roles in all parts of Roma Novan life, including that of ruler.

But like their ancestors, the 11th century Roma Novans have determination, war-fighting skills and engineering genius. Outside the usual circles of alliances, they often act as intermediaries, overtly and covertly. They know other people's secrets...

Currently living under the shadow of the Eastern Roman Empire (the Byzantine Empire as we know it), Roma Nova dances carefully, but sometimes has to give in to its much larger cousin. Hence the presence of Countess Galla Mitela, chief advisor to the imperatrix of Roma Nova, at the court of William of Normandy. Could these tough, strange people negotiate between Saxon England and Normandy, appointed Harold and ambitious William? And did they have an alternative plan?

'Gods, Galla, how long are we going to be stuck in this cursed boat?'

I stood in the prow and looked down at my cousin huddling in her misery. She'd puked all the way across the British Sea to Gaul and almost all the way down the Sequana river that the Normans called the Seine. Poor child. Claudia was only seventeen and hated going out on the river at home.

'Not long now. The shipmaster assures me we'll reach Rotomagus this afternoon.' No, Rou-en. Gods, it sounded like a donkey braying.

It was only the fourth day since we'd left the harbour near Magnus Portus now the Saxon port of Bosham. We'd headed across the choppy water for Gesoriacum, once the proud home of the Roman Classis Britannica, the vital link between Gaul and Britannia. As we'd sailed past, it looked like a scruffy little hole in the wall, its dock half silted up. Well, its function as northern fleet headquarters had been over six centuries ago. What had I expected? Little had been built since our ancestors left Gaul. We'd sailed further south down the coast, passing the wide bay of the Samara. The salt tang of the open sea was invaded by the smell of brackish marshes. Screwing my eyes up and peering across the wide, open expanse of the flatlands, I'd seen a group of tiny warships bobbing in the water in the natural harbour. They were making their way towards us, the harbour mouth and ultimately the open sea. But we passed by before they came anywhere near us.

I shivered in the chill July morning and drew my cloak round me. Instead of the pale breaking light of a clear sky heralding a fair summer's day, it was misty and overcast again. Our Saxon escort from the ship fyrd left us, setting off for the safety of England before we entered the mouth of the Sequana. We sailed past a boatyard on the south bank too frantic with activity even at that hour to notice another foreign trading ship. Tents and ramshackle huts clustered around a village the shipmaster called Hunefloth. I could hear the clanging of metal upon metal across the open water.

We sailed upriver only passing the occasional small vessel dwarfed by our trader; the land either side was mostly wooded interspersed with fields and peasants' cottages. No farms or villas, just the occasional jetty or mooring point. As we rounded the steep headland dominated by the castle of Robert the Devil, I wondered what kind of reception we would get at Rotomagus.

We'd left the Saxon port with many good wishes for our travels, food and wine for our journey and a sad smile from one particular warrior on the quayside. Eadmær. I grasped the wooden rail harder. I'd watched until his tall figure had diminished to a blur. If we failed, I would never see him again. If we succeeded, he was his king's man and would never come back with me to Roma Nova. I released my breath.

'Still dreaming of your yellow-haired Saxon?' Claudia gave me a knowing look. 'Is he blond all over his body?'

I felt the warmth crawling up my neck into my face. 'No concern of yours, child. Be silent.' I frowned at her.

'I'm not a child and you can't talk to me in that way. You might be the senior countess and my mother's chief advisor, but I'm her daughter and heir!'

'Then behave like it. The imperatrix would be ashamed of your behaviour.'

She shrugged and turned her back to me and pretended to study the scenery. She sulked until we rounded the last bend in the Sequana and saw our destination. A small town on a flat river plain, based on the earlier walled *castrum*, squatted against wooded hills. As we approached the mooring point to the west away from the shallow channels and low islands, we could see work parties labouring to build a more formal quayside. On deck, our servants busied themselves preparing our bundles for disembarkation to smaller boats which would take us to the solid ground of the town. Claudia leaned towards me.

'Aren't we going to change?'

'There's nothing wrong with how we are dressed,' I replied. 'We are as we are.' We wore practical wool tunics over linen shirts, trousers, long boots and wool hooded cloaks. Both of us had tied our hair back in a single long plait, although Claudia's curly brown hair sprang away and framed her face. And we'd taken the precaution of wearing our imperial badges.

'*Domina.*' The Praetorian centurion nodded his head in the direction of a small boat coming towards us. I leaned over the side and watched as two men scrambled up the rope ladder one of our sailors had let down.

The first over the rail was a dark-haired, close-shaven sturdy man who had little trouble heaving himself on board. He was followed by a slighter man who had hitched his long tunic up into his belt to scale the side and fidgeted as he smoothed it back down. His head was shaved on the crown; a priest. The first man, dressed in a maroon tunic with embroidered edging, and a silver belt, cast around, passed over Claudia and me and addressed himself to the centurion.

'I am Gilbert de Boscville,' he said, to the centurion. 'Where is your commander?' he asked in Latin with an accent so thick I could barely understand.

The Saxons had warned us about de Boscville; he was one of Duke William's close aides, a harsh ruler of his lands and fiercely loyal to his master. I nodded to the centurion, who drew back.

'I am Galla Mitela, imperial councillor and Countess of the South, leading the Roma Nova delegation,' I began. 'May I present Claudia Apulia, daughter and heir of Imperatrix—'

'Where is the commander?' he interrupted and waved impatiently.

The servants froze. Some gasped. The centurion drew his sword and closed the gap between Claudia and de Boscville. The remaining Praetorians took a step closer to me.

De Boscville frowned, but stepped back at the centurion's fierce glare.

'My Lord de Boscville, you are insolent as well as ignorant,' I said in my coldest voice. 'Have the goodness to wait until I have finished speaking. And listen to each word carefully.'

Claudia stared at me. Perhaps she had never heard me reprimand anybody so severely.

De Boscville flushed and the features on his dark face drew closer.

'I do not deal with *women*. Where is the senior man? I am to escort him and his delegation to my lord duke.'

'Then you are destined to be disappointed. He does not exist.' I flicked my hand impatiently. 'Are we to remain here all night waiting on your dignity? If Duke William does not wish to hear the latest news from England, then we will set sail now.' I turned and waved to the shipmaster. 'Plot a course downriver away from this barbarian place and find us a berth for the night. Tomorrow we return to Roma Nova.'

'At once, *domina*.' He bowed and hurried off waving arms and shouting.

'The Praetorians will see you off my ship, Lord de Boscville, or you will be sailing with us.' I turned my back on him and grasped Claudia's arm.

'What are you doing?' she hissed at me as we entered the little cabin amidships.

'Tactics, my girl. You wait and see.'

'But Mother will kill you if you don't see the duke. She says you have to stop this war.'

'We'll see him, don't worry.' I smiled to myself and counted the heartbeats that passed.

Five minutes later, we were climbing down the rope ladder to the small boat waiting below. We'd declined the sling usually used for 'ladies'. De Boscville scowled in silence, forced to have acknowledged us. To be truthful, he looked ill. As the boat bobbed in the water, I smiled graciously at the priest who promptly crossed himself, no doubt warding himself against the pagan Romans. On the riverside, a troop of horsemen were waiting for us with spare mounts. Their captain looked at de Boscville, a question on his face.

'You can ride, I assume?' he said.

I said nothing, but Claudia and I swung up onto the two tallest horses in reply. The six Praetorians were given mounts and fell in behind us, immediately in front of de Boscville's men.

'Pray lead on, my lord,' I said in my most condescending tone and nodded. He grunted and led off.

'Well, it's comfortable enough, but not warm,' Claudia said. She fidgeted on a velvet covered padded stool as my body servant teased her curly hair up into an intricate pattern of plaits holding her diadem secure. I pressed my hand onto her shoulder.

'Sit still, child, and let Marcia do her work.' I draped her wool *stola* across her shoulders. 'We have to look as imposing as possible. The duke is a hard man, but apparently impressed by ceremony. That is why you must wear gold in your hair and purple on your back.'

'But I don't understand why you are wearing your Praetorian *lorica*.' She ran her eye down my figure. Like hers, my hair was bound up in classic Roman style, but plainer. Over a dark green tunic which nearly reached the floor but didn't cover my senator's red boots, I wore Praetorian *lorica hamata*, the chain mail shirt complete with *phalerae* I'd earned. I'd tied a simple black knotted legionary's *focale* around my neck against the draughts. Hung across my shoulders was the gold chain collar with the Mitela badge decorated with myrtle leaf and eagle enamel. And whatever de Boscville had said about bearing arms in the castle, my *gladius* was firmly attached at the left to my gold and leather belt along with a ceremonial *pugio* dagger on the right. The combined weight was not inconsiderable. I'd chosen a dark green cloak pinned with a chased gold fibula my mother had given my when I became an imperial councillor. I touched it for luck. May her spirit and Juno guide me tonight.

A knock on the door interrupted my thoughts and my answer to Claudia. The Praetorian commander and his troop waited in formation in the corridor. The flickering torches in the wall sconces reflected on their polished helmets. I held my hand out to Claudia.

'Come, *principissa*.'

'Don't call me by that stupid name, Galla. That's what *he* calls me.' Her face flushed red with anger. I pressed her fingers in sympathy and kept my own sourness inside. 'He', or as I called him in my head 'that Eastern bastard', was Claudia's mother's companion, Gregory. He'd arrived two years ago from Constantinople, the son of the late emperor Constantine Monomachos, and had spent that time worming his way into the imperatrix's favour. He was behind me being sent on this mission, cozening the imperatrix, saying I was equipped with unique statecraft gifts and experience to mediate between Saxons and Northmen. As her chief advisor, I was obviously in his way in his quest for power. Roma Nova had been pressured by the Eastern Roman emperor to mediate between Normandy and England: the Saxons were valuable trading partners for them as well as for Roma Nova. Although many Norman mercenaries served the Eastern Empire's military forces, the emperor was wary of their expansion into Italy. The Norman warriors were fierce, efficient and usually victorious. Nothing seemed to stop them; perhaps it was the wolfish Viking blood that ran in their veins. If Normandy won England and dominated the North their power would increase considerably.

Unfortunately, Gregory had been present when the imperatrix had received the messenger from Constantinople. Lost in the joys of forthcoming late motherhood, she had nodded her head to his suggestion and I was dispatched. I was caught for now by the imperatrix's command, but when I returned, things would change.

'I apologise, *domina*,' I said, and bowed to her daughter in front of me. Claudia frowned, then broke into a wide smile. Now engulfed in her purple wool *stola*, she must have felt the chill from the stone walls less. But her sandaled feet must have frozen on the stone slabs. She grasped my hand, straightened her back and we set off.

The ducal palace built by Duke William's father was imposing; the stone tower dominated but as we were shown into the *Aula Turris*, the *Grande Salle*, I was struck not only by the heat but also by the sheer luxury of its proportions and decoration. Here ruled a man of power indeed. At the top of the walls ran a blind arcade of semi-circular arches under which were hangings of rich reds, blues and greens, some embroidered with gold and silver thread. But even richer were the gowns and jewelled belts of the women in the hall and the tunics and mantles of their men. And at the far end on a raised dais were William and Matilda. A slim figure, her eyes were full of curiosity. Like the other women present her hair was hidden beneath a veil below a gold circlet, but of such softness it could only have been the nearly sheer silk from Constantinople. But William had none of the delicate elegance of his wife. From the heavy gold circle with a large cabochon shining from its centre on his head, down the dark crimson robe and over mantle clothing his sturdy frame, belted by gold, down to his dark boots, he exuded wealth and strength. His eyes fixed on us from the moment we stood on the threshold of the hall until we reached the two thrones where they sat.

'*Salvete dux ducissaque,*' I began. William frowned, but Matilda smiled although she said nothing. De Boscville stepped out of the lines of courtiers, his face creased in irritation. He translated my greeting into French, then turned and said in Latin, 'Continue.'

'Forgive me, Duke William,' I said in French. I paused and smiled. 'I had not realised you did not speak Latin.'

William frowned again and shot a hard look at me. I knew perfectly well he couldn't even read or write his own native tongue.

'I present Claudia Apulia,' I said. 'She brings greeting from her mother, the imperatrix of Roma Nova.'

He nodded curtly and stared her up and down like a piece of meat. She flushed slightly, but looked back steadily at him. Matilda laid her fingers on his forearm.

'We have been asked to convey a message to you from Harold the Saxon King.'

'The only message I want from the *earl* is the surrender of my rightful crown.'

'That, Duke William, is not for negotiation.' Some of the courtiers present murmured, and one man, another priest who I thought must be Lanfranc, his Galilean councillor, bent and whispered in the duke's ear. I waited until the murmuring had stopped and I had their attention again. 'Harold does not wish for warfare, but as you know from his campaign against the Welsh, he will not hesitate to enter the field in force if England is threatened. He proposes a treaty, starting with a calming period over the winter.'

'He is forsworn. That is an end on it. You are women but even you as Romans understand an oath is an oath.'

'Of course, but some would say he swore under duress.'

'You push too hard, woman.'

'I merely state the obvious, Duke.'

'We will think about it.'

'All the while you are mustering your invasion fleet?'

The murmuring rose to a clamour. Somebody muttered 'godless bitches'. Claudia took a sharp breath in at that but we stood still and waited.

'Peace!' the duke's voice rang out. 'The countess and princess are our guests. We will eat.' He stood and beckoned me to accompany him, Matilda smiled at Claudia, took her arm and followed us, the courtiers trailing in our wake.

A hard, uncompromising man with few social manners but willing to talk of common interests, he was deeply interested in how Roma Nova had been founded and in my own early career, sword in hand. I think he almost forgot I was a woman as we discussed campaigns and tactics. His eyes gleamed when I showed him the intricately worked *pugio* dagger. His acquisitiveness wasn't merely for a crown.

'Please accept it as a gift, Duke,' I said. 'Whatever happens in the future, it will be a souvenir of the Romans who once visited you.'

'I accept, most willingly.' He gave a half-smile. 'But you will not cozen me with your words and gifts.'

'I regret we cannot convince you of a peaceful way. I urge you to reconsider the advantages of a treaty. It will bring you more security in the end.'

'As your people have found.' He gave me a sardonic look. 'But you are now at the beck and call of the Greeks in the East.'

I bit my lip. 'Only for the moment, Duke. Sometimes, we have to endure discomfort for the sake of peace. The Eastern Romans have many troubles and have lost the earlier resolution of the times of Constantine. Roma Nova may yet outlive them.'

'Ha!' He searched my face while a servant refilled my

cup. 'You are a strong woman, Countess, but why are you here? Should you not be tending your family?'

'I am the imperatrix's chief councillor, Duke. My children are grown and my life is given to the service of my ruler.'

I dismissed the body servants and combed Claudia's hair out myself. I needed to move my shoulders and arms after shedding the weight of my *lorica*.

'Did Matilda say anything interesting to you?'

'She is devoted to the duke, she busies herself with her children, their contracted marriages, her devotion to the Galilean god, her temple building projects.' Claudia twisted round. 'She has a lively mind and sees everything, but although rich and admired, she has no purpose beyond that. I think she frets about the duke and his obsession with England. But she is a conventional wife and will not question his actions.'

'So we cannot influence him via that route.' I stopped and laid my hands on Claudia's shoulders. She looked into the polished surface of her mirror.

'Did Mama give you any other orders?'

'Yes, but they may put us in danger.'

'But we must still follow them.'

'Yes. You are growing up too fast, Claudia Apulia.'

'No faster than any of our ancestors, Galla.'

Duke William was occupied inspecting an important building today, de Boscville announced to me as we broke bread the next morning. I glanced at him, but his harsh features revealed nothing. I suspected the 'building' under inspection would be naval rather than stone. The duchess had invited us to sit with her and the other women until the evening when his master would give me his formal answer.

'Claudia Apulia would be delighted to accept,' I said, ignoring Claudia's look of surprise swiftly followed by one of annoyance. 'However, I would, with Duchess Matilda's permission, like to visit Iuliobona – Lillebonne.'

'Why?'

'Pure sentiment. One of my ancestors was stationed there as a tribune and wrote an account of his time. It was an important and wealthy regional centre as well as a port to Britannia. I should like to see the remains. I believe the theatre was a fine one which could seat three thousand.' I smiled at him, but he frowned back. He was the surliest man I had ever met.

We jogged along the dirt road on good strong mounts, de Boscville and I, followed by two Praetorians and two of his men-at-arms. He'd insisted on accompanying me; I didn't know whether as guard or escort. It would be his misfortune if he became weary inspecting the relics of past times that meant nothing to him. His ancestors were probably scratching around northern mountains eating raw fish they'd caught that morning or hunched in smelly huts round an open fire while mine ruled the known world.

After a midday meal in a tavern where de Boscville's autocratic manner secured us a table and good if terrified service, I asked to see the commercial part of the town. I smiled when I saw the main street of shops and stalls was called the Rue des Césars, presumably the Decumanus Maximus of old Iuliobona. I was looking for a cloth merchant; the wool here had an excellent reputation and would make a suitable gift for the imperatrix. But that wasn't the only reason I stopped in front of one timber-framed building.

Inside, the merchant showed us bolts of fine and sturdy cloth dyed in various colours.

'We have colleagues from England, my lady, with some of their special South Downs wool cloth.' He ushered me towards the far side of his hall where a young man stood folding a length of rich copper-coloured stuff. Behind the table, all I could see of his companion was the top of his blond head as he made marks on a wax tablet. He looked up at my approach and I halted in my tracks. Eadmær. He stared hard at me, almost frowning. I didn't say his name aloud, but my heart thudded. What in the depths of Tartarus was *he* doing here, right under the nose of William's people and obviously in disguise?

I glanced at de Boscville who sat at the side, drinking the merchant's ale, tapping his fingers on his thigh as I made my choices. I fingered some of the cloth as if considering purchasing it but couldn't stop looking at Eadmær. I lowered my voice and asked the merchant for the privy. His wife led me down a narrow passageway to the back door giving onto the courtyard.

I slumped against the back of the building to catch my breath for a moment and steady my heart. I thought Eadmær safe in England. If de Boscville even suspected one of Harold's most faithful aides was only a few steps away... As I turned in the direction the merchant's wife indicated, hands grabbed me and pulled me behind the privy hut.

'I thought you would never arrive,' Eadmær whispered.

'What in Hades are you doing here?' I hissed back.

He grinned at me. 'I put myself forward to lead the clandestine group.'

'But you're no common spy!'

'Ah, Galla, my Galla. I had to see you again.' He pulled me to him, his arm encircling my waist. The warmth of his body almost overwhelmed me and I closed my eyes. His lips touched mine and I opened them to receive his kiss.

'My lady?' came the merchant's wife's voice. She bustled over to the hut. Eadmær scuttled round the side. I nearly laughed at his expression of alarm.

'Thank you, goodwife, I will be another moment,' I said and fiddled with my belt. As soon as she'd disappeared through the back door of the house, he grabbed me by the arm.

'Quickly, give me the news.'

'William is determined, almost obsessed. He is building ships day and night. You must prepare strong defences at sea and on the coast.'

'We will fight him with every sinew to the last drop of blood.'

'Very noble, but how many will die?'

'I care not how many of *them* fall. Englishmen will sacrifice themselves if it stops the damned Normans from seizing our island.'

'Gods, Eadmær, why do you men see fighting as the only solution?'

'What? Is this a Roman speaking? Are you only a woman after all?' His fingers ran down my cheek and I shivered at his touch.

'It would be better for all if his ships never set sail,' I retorted.

'Why in Pluto's balls' name are we crouching in this blasted hedge?' Claudia whispered.

'Language, child,' I murmured, but I was concentrating on the harbour below us and trying to count the hundreds of ships bobbing below. The shipyard singing with the noise of hammering and sawing was guarded, torches flared everywhere, peasants were loading supplies, men-at-arms and horses crowding and champing on the makeshift quayside. A pity so many people and animals were present.

The day before, we'd made formal farewells and sailed from Rotomagus with false smiles and regret on both sides, but I'd ordered the sailing master of our trading ship to stop briefly downriver near the harbour serving Iuliobona to pick up Eadmær and his men. Their dozen and our ten

Praetorians along with Claudia and myself should manage the task if we applied ourselves.

Claudia and I had crawled back about twenty feet from the cliff edge when I heard something move. The creak of a boot. I made a sharp cutting gesture and she froze. Young though she was, like all Romans over sixteen Claudia was trained in basic warrior skills. There, again, metal rubbing on cloth. The clink of metal on metal. Eadmær and his men were in the valley. If he'd come to join us, he would have whistled the signal. There was no whistle.

I gestured Claudia to crawl directly to the side and edged away on my belly in the opposite direction. Perhaps it was only peasants marauding for food or loot. I eased my *gladius* out, then in the shelter of a low shrub came to a crouch. Then I saw them. A group of three horsemen; one dismounted, knelt and examined the ground.

'Well?' A bad-tempered voice.

De Boscville.

'Somebody was here, lord, recently.'

'That damned Roman woman, I'd wager.'

'But they've sailed, haven't they?'

'Supposedly. The duke thinks their threats to hinder our trade were bluster and they can do nothing, but she's a devious bitch.'

'Look, there!' The other horseman pointed in Claudia's direction. The clouds had parted and the damned moon shone through. Pluto swive him. I stood.

'My Lord de Boscville,' I said. 'What brings you out here at this time of night?'

'Seize her!'

I ran, but even the fastest human couldn't beat a warhorse. De Boscville charged and swung at me with his longsword. As I rolled away, he leapt off his horse and, face working in fury, ran at me. He raised his sword aloft, but I ducked under his arm and, crouching low, thrust into his groin, then leapt aside and struck into his side. His sword caught my left arm as it fell, numbing it for an instant. De Boscville was on the ground grunting and struggling to stand. My breath was heaving, as hard as my heart hammered. I whirled round to find the tracker on me. I shoved him away, jabbing him in the stomach, then the throat. He clasped his hands to his face with a cry and fell. The thunder of the third rider's horse was ringing in my head as I turned to face him. I had no breath to run. The horse reared to crush me and I faced death. Then the animal collapsed and the rider fell. Claudia stood there, trembling, blood running down her *gladius* and tears down her face. The horse whinnied piteously. She'd severed its tendons. The rider was unconscious.

I swallowed hard.

'Dispatch the animal.' She stared at me. I nodded. She knelt and drew the blade across the horse's throat. Then she turned round and was violently sick.

De Boscville struggled, but he was mortally wounded.

'Peace, man, prepare to meet your god.'

'You—' he gasped. 'Knew you were poison. Told duke.'

'No, we came to stop you waging a war of aggression, of conquest against a nation that has done you no harm.'

'William has right. Harold forsworn.' He winced. 'For God and Christ.' His head fell to one side and he passed into the shades.

'There are several hundred ships, some half complete, others bobbing in the water.' I stopped to draw breath and gulp down ale from the flask Eadmær thrust at me.

'How many hundred?' He frowned at me.

'Four or five at least.'

'Christ good Jesu, we could never match that many ships! And how can we, less than a score, hope to destroy even a portion of them?'

'Your men can all shoot straight, can't they?'

'That is a foolish question, Galla.'

'Very well.'

The Saxons crouched in an arc near the edge of the cliff watching the Praetorians ready their portable *manuballistae*. I nodded at the Praetorian commander who instructed his *optio* to distribute boxes of arrows with narrow tubes along the shafts to Eadmær's men.

'What are these?' he ran his fingers along the tubes.

I flinched. 'Do not play with them. They are not always stable, but once loosed, they will achieve our aim.' A cold wave rolled through me, but I had to give the order.

Together the loaded arrows and bolts rained down destruction that scorched and burnt, that even danced across the water. White flames of death burst out engulfing the boats, the quay and, Juno save us, the living creatures fleeing from the boats.

'Christ's breath, what is that, Galla?' Eadmær looked aghast at the intensity with which everything below us was consumed. The thunder of explosions and screams reached us across the clear night.

'*Ignis graecus* – Greek fire. A terrible weapon.'

I shut my eyes after ten minutes, weary of death and destruction.

'Now we must sail from here as if the Furies themselves were pursuing us. Come.' I took his hand and pulled him away. 'Sometimes we must do dreadful acts to prevent greater disasters, but at least history will record that the Galilean year of 1066 was not the one in which Northman William invaded Saxon England.'

AUTHOR'S NOTE

Language: As Latin speakers, the Roma Novans use the same Latin place names as their ancestors did. Sequana (fluvius) is the River Seine, Samara (fluvius) the River Somme, Gesoriacum was the Roman naval port at

Boulogne, Magnus Portus became Bosham, Rotomagus Rouen, Iuliobona Lillebonne. Just for neatness, the port of Hunefloth was the early Norman French name for Honfleur.

The Roma Novans, who worshipped the traditional gods, called Christians 'Galileans' as the revered Julian the Philosopher did.

Roma Novans still wore chain mail overshirts – the *lorica hamata* – and wielded a *gladius* (short sword) and *pugio* (dagger). *Phalerae* were the equivalent of medals and a *focale* was a simple scarf worn around a legionary's neck. *Manuballistae* were portable bolt throwing weapons, roughly equivalent to crossbows.

Alison Morton
www.alison-morton.com

DISCUSSION SUGGESTIONS

What would Europe – the world – be like if Rome had survived?

In the Monty Python movie 'Life Of Brian' there is a famous scene about 'What have the Romans ever done for us?' So what *did* the Romans do for us?

AUGUST

1066

*W*illiam's ships were built in all the major ports along Normandy's considerable coastline, but the large majority seem to have gathered at Dives, just north of William's western stronghold of Caen. At some point in late August they set sail. Nobody knows exactly why.

What we do know is that most of them ended up at St Valery, from where William eventually launched his invasion in late September. This may have been a planned move, for St Valery was an ancient Roman port and may well have had docks suitable for easily loading horses into ships. But it is also possible that there was an initial invasion attempt... that went very wrong.

Even if this was the case, we still do not know if it went wrong because of contrary winds, storms in the Narrow Sea, or an encounter with English ships – which also, around this time, seem to have left their station on the Isle of Wight and returned to harbour in the Thames with significant losses...

IN THE WAKE OF THE DOLPHIN
Helen Hollick

Adapted from chapters of *Harold the King* (UK title)
I Am the Chosen King (US title)

When the wind shifted further to the south, with his English navy, the schypfyrd, waiting near the Isle of Wight, Harold knew things might, at last, begin to happen. There was a new uprush of expectation among the men. Daggers were eased loose, hands gripped tighter on the oars of the warships – the sturdy thirty-two and forty-oared Dragon Craft. All eyes were keening southwards. Towards Normandy.

The English spies knew how many ships Duke William had mustered, how many – how few – would be under oar, showing that he was no sea warrior. The majority of William's fleet relied on sail, requiring a fair-set wind to accompany them across the ninety-odd miles between Dives-sur-Mer and... and where? That, the English spies could not discover, only conjecture; and that too, might depend on the fickleness of the wind. Once he set sail, William could beach anywhere along the English coast. He had to be stopped before then – and the English were good at blockading against sea-borne attack.

Cursing the poor sea conditions, Duke William would also have been waiting and watching, ready to set sail with his fleet. All summer men had been watching the weather, waiting...

At last, one day in mid-August, the wind changed...

Eadric the Steersman stood, eyes squinting into the brightness, balancing with the lift and fall of *Dolphin*'s foredeck, his head up, nostrils scenting the sea wind as if he were a wolf seeking prey. They were all one of the pack, these English sailors, waiting to be loosed for the hunt. All they needed was a sight of the enemy to start the run. King Harold was relying heavily on his fleet commander's instinct and great knowledge. The movements of tide and wind were family to Eadric, being mother, daughter, wife and mistress. He knew all its moods, its tempers and subtleties. His senses told him that William's fleet was coming. He could not see sail or wave-thresh, but they were there, heading northward. Had anyone asked, Eadric would have answered that he could smell them, as an animal would smell an approaching storm. His bones felt them. Or at least, if William had not ordered his men to sea, then he was a fool – for this was ideal weather. If it held.

Eadric bit his lower lip, deep in thought. Would this wind hold? Or would she, capricious as she had been all summer long, swing back to her previous hunting run across the Great Sea to the west? If Eadric could not decide the mood of the wind, then neither, he doubted, would William's sailors. Had the Duke of Normandy committed himself to action or was he dithering? Was the pricking of Eadric's skin, the tingling behind his neck, playing him for the fool? Happen they had all been on edge too long during this frustrating summer's wait!

The Norman army was growing restless, this much England knew as fact; supplies were diminishing, the eagerness for adventure dwindling into exasperation. Waiting for the wind was a desperate occupation. Hah! Duke William ought to have used oar, not sail! With oar they would already be here – but then, with oar, the Duke would have needed to find the men to row, or the time to teach such men the skill. That was a thing the King, Harold, had told Eadric of William's nature. He was not a man to bide his time, to be patient, to wait and wait again until the thing slid right, into place.

A voice, distant but clear, sounded from *Dolphin*'s steerboard side; Eadric swung round, questioning, then raised his hand in acknowledgement to Bjarni Redbeard from the *Sea Star*, a craft that matched the length and speed of *Dolphin*. Eadric cupped his hands around his mouth and shouted back; 'Nay! I see nothing – but they are there, mark you. I know they are there!'

'Aye, we all feel it! He would be moon-mad, I am thinking, to pass by this opportunity.'

Bjarni was about to say more, but his shout was abruptly silenced for the horn sounded, distant, from the south, from where *Wave Dancer* was patrolling. All the men came alert, breath held, listening. Again, the long mournful cry of the war horn… and a third time.

Eadric himself was the first to break the enchantment. He leapt, in four strides, from stern to mast, took up *Dolphin*'s own long and curving aurochs' horn, and blew three blasts in response. The sound scudded over the creaming waves, was caught by the wind and lifted to the high clouds. In that instant, the men, too, had come alive, racing for the rowing benches. Hands tight-gripping the oars their heads turned, expectant, towards Eadric their master, awaiting his signal.

For a long moment he stood there amidships, fists bunched against his hips, legs spread, feeling the eager roll of his tight-held ship. The salt taste of the sea stung against his lips, the song of the wind whistled past his ears. His attention snatched to a white wake that folded around the hull – and another, and another. A silver glistening back; a fin…

He pointed and laughed, 'Look, my brothers!' he crowed, 'we have our friends to accompany us as we go to meet this bastard Duke of Normandy! Look! The dolphins have come to run with their sister!'

A shout of exultation was tossed to the height of the mast, the strain was taken up by arm muscles, and Eadric shouted the command they had so eagerly awaited.

'*Lift her*! *Lift her*!'

Dolphin and *Sea Star* began to glide forward through the

choppy sea. From the west, the answering *boom* and *boom* of the war horns from *Moon Crest* and *Sun Singer*. From the east, *Cloud Chaser* and *Gull*. From behind, *Shape Shifter, Sea Eagle* and *Red Sail;* from ahead, *Wind Whisperer, Wave Prancer* and *Spindrift*… from more and more of the fleet: *Sword Song, Tern, Breeze, Hawk*…

The wolf pack was loose, and running fast towards the Chase and the Kill.

Like most of them crammed tight into the ships, Duke William was no sailor, but at least the strong wine he had swallowed before embarkation was keeping his belly where it ought to be – unlike many of the men who were hanging over the sides, spewing up their guts. How the horses were faring he could only guess, but at least the sea had calmed its heaving once they had cleared the coast of Cap d'Antifer. That had been one of the most terrifying ordeals of his entire life – and he had endured plenty. He had hidden his fear from the men as the boat had leapt, tossed and bucked, his fear heightened because he had no control over the ship, the sea, or the wind. A wind that was not blowing from as far south as they would have liked, but the decision to risk setting sail had to be made. They had already waited over long, and the opportunity, so William had been reliably advised by his seafarers, might not come again.

'What are our chances?' William had asked as they had gathered together in a solemn group outside his command tent, his thumb rubbing over the ruby set within his ducal ring. Some, not willing to commit themselves, had scratched at neck and cheek, fiddled with ear lobes. Others had slowly shaken their heads, but most had agreed that the wind was unlikely to prove kinder this side of autumn. Clearing that lee shore was the dilemma. If only the wind would back a little more! Dives, the majority had confirmed, was not the most favourable place from which to launch a fleet. This prevailing wind was too westward, the lee shore too hazardous. Further along the coast would have been better – Eu, perhaps? Closer, too, to England.

This particular argument had swung, blade about hilt, throughout the year, but William had been adamant. His muster point was Dives, closer to his favourite town, Caen. Mile upon mile of sand suitable for the building of ships, and the encampment of men. Beyond, sufficient grazing for horses. Higher up the coast would mean a shorter, quicker voyage, but what was nearer for William was nearer for Harold. His English fleet was more capable at sea, his spies were efficient. Dives-sur-Mer was more protected because of its distance. *Non*, William was determined. When Harold learnt of Norman manoeuvring, it would be too late. The invasion fleet would be almost upon him.

The captains had been right about that lee shore, however.

William stood at the prow of his command ship, *Mora*, his fingernails digging into the wood of the curving bulwark. He closed his eyes, saw again the spew of wave foam against rock and cliff, heard in his ears the rush of the sea as it had beat against that rock-lined stretch of coast. The ships' masters had known what they were doing, the wind had held, and all but three ships of the convoy had slipped past those dangerous currents and headed out into the open sea. But that still meant the loss of three ships – and all the men and equipment they carried.

They were almost halfway across, so *Mora*'s commander had said. So far, all had gone to plan, even allowing for those rocks and the few difficult horses that had been abandoned at Dives or had their throats cut, their blood-spilling carcasses heaved overboard. The mood of the men was buoyant and eager after these weeks within the confines of the camp. A few more weeks and William would not have been certain of holding their loyalty. Loading the supplies had taken much of their attention, but once that had been completed there was nothing to do save wait. No matter, now, they were under way, the thresh of spindrift frothing the water into a white churn of spray, curving beneath the bows of more than seven hundred ships.

William gazed with pride at the array: large, sturdy traders' craft, smaller fishing boats, a handful of warships, all held in tight check so as not to outrun the slower vessels. So many of them! Patterned sails, plain, striped, patched; red, blue, white, green, brown and saffron. Some men in the next ship saw their duke watching them, raised their arms in salute and cheered his presence.

Content, he saluted back.

His own vessel was superb, a Flemish warship given as a gift by his wife, built and paid for from her own purse. He glanced up at the wide billow of her striped red and saffron square sail, the bronze crucifix at the masthead glinting in the late afternoon sunlight. Come nightfall, a lantern would be raised, as there would on all the boats to enable them to keep together – at least until any damned English ships were sighted. To avoid them, he was relying on the skill of his own Norman warships, riding ahead. They must discover the waiting English, signal word so that lanterns could be covered, sails reefed, course altered... Over seven hundred vessels to be brought through a blockade under the secrecy of darkness. They had assured him it could be done, his captains and sea commanders. If they kept their nerve and their wit, they had said.

If.

The Duke raised his head, sniffed at the salt wind. The sun was dipping towards the western horizon. An hour until dusk. One more hour. Come dawn, pray God, they should be seeing the grey outline of England's southern coast.

The Normans heard the hollow boom of the war horns before they saw the indistinct shadow-shape of ships. The white of oar stroke and bow wave, the gleam of bronze and glint of gold reflecting the sinking sun from the carved, grinning heads of the curving prows. Dragons, wing-stretched ravens, sea monsters. At their head, a craft with a prow shaped as a leaping dolphin. The English schypfyrd; the sea wolf warriors.

Duke William watched in morbid fascination as they approached, racing through the waves. So fast did they fly from the strengthening dusk – even against the wind, but then, they were powered by thirty, forty, fifty, oars and were carried by the run of the tide. Eight knots or so could they speed across the open sea under the power of those oars, he had been told – by whom and when, he could not recall. He could see the bank of oars to either side of the dolphin ship; could hear, now, the shouts echoing across the expanse of water between them, an expanse that was rapidly narrowing. Could hear, but not understand the meaning.

'What is it they shout?'

'It is the steersman, lord, calling the beat of the oar.'

Unaware that he had spoken aloud, William stared at the man behind him who had spoken, a Flemish sailor.

'And what ought we do about them?' William asked caustically.

The sailor shrugged, pointed vaguely at the sails of the Norman fleet. 'We do as the others are already doing, my lord. We turn about and run. Or we drop to our knees and pray.'

The blood-anger streamed to William's face, his breathing came in rasping gasps from his throat. 'I run from nothing and no one!' The words burst from his mouth as his strides took him aft to where his captain stood, issuing a burst of orders to the crew.

'We fight!' William bellowed, his fists clenched. 'Give the order on the horn – set ready the archers. We fight!'

'*Non!*' *Mora*'s captain countermanded. 'Your warships that were ahead must surely have already been destroyed. Your fleet is made of merchant vessels for sailing not for fighting; when such encounter pirates, they flee. It is not prudent to fight one of those dragon ships – and besides, our luck is turning against us twice over. See our sail, my lord? It is flapping. The wind has cast against us. She is veering to the west.'

Normandy's proud and glorious fleet began to scatter in disarray. Each ship, careless now of keeping within the discipline of the convoy, broke free and fled before the westering wind. Better, the seamen all agreed, to turn for Normandy than meet the fire arrows of the English. All except Duke William, who stood rigid in the stern of his ship, with no choice but to watch.

As well the words that ran through his mind were not voiced, for his oaths would have startled even sea-tainted sailors.

Four-and-twenty ships obeyed their duke's command to sail onward. Four-and-twenty out of seven hundred. They held his best soldiers, his archers, his swordsmen. They grouped together, the sailors doing their best to steer, to control rudder and sail; the Norman soldiers did their best to prepare to fight. But how could those who had never fought from the rolling, heaving, deck of a ship, fight? Their armour was too heavy, their weapons too cumbersome, their legs not seaworthy. How could men, used to fighting from the back of a warhorse, learn, within the space of a matter of a few heartbeats, how to protect their very lives from the experience of men who had been born to the ways of the sea?

How could these Norman men know what to do when English fire-arrows arced through the dusk sky that was fading from the golds and crimsons of a vivid sunset, into the purples and dark blue hues of the night? Streaking like the breath of outraged dragons, the fire came, and the black smoke billowed.

The Duke stood in the prow, stood stunned, numb of voice and movement. Stood there seeing, feeling, nothing. The screams of men, his men, his Norman men, filled his ears, but he heard not a sound. His eyes saw the ships, one by one, become engulfed in flame, saw men, also so engulfed, leap into the water. Watched them burn, watched them drown – yet saw… nothing.

Mora shuddered as a series of fire-arrows struck her. Her tarred hull and single tar-grimed canvas sail burst into flame, the caulking between her decking running with spreading fire. William stood there, mesmerised, as the runnels of flame tore towards him. He heard his ship groan, cry out, as the stays holding her mast upright snapped, the whiplash sound of their parting tearing through the air, loud above the roar of shouting, screams, and the burning crackle of fire.

She sank, stern first. He did nothing to save himself. Nothing at all.

One ship was spared. One, single, Norman ship.

'Tell them in Normandy,' Eadric the Steersman shouted as the first stars witnessed the night, and what was left of the burning destruction floating as debris among the rolling waves. 'Tell them to not dare, ever again, to wake the dragon that is the schypfyrd of England!'

He signalled for the war horns to sound the order for

the fleet to begin the long, slow, row back to England. A long journey, but a glorious one.

That one reprieved ship took aboard all the men she could, those men who knew enough to kick with their feet, or grasp floating debris in order to stay alive, to not drown. As full night fell, the stars peered from behind wisps of cloud like a scatter of jewels spread across the black, black sky, indifferent to the single ship below. The steersman, bone weary, devastated – frightened – allowed one last man to be hauled aboard; they could not take any more, for overladen the ship would sink, but then, there were no more to save. There was no comfort to offer, no blankets, no food, little fresh water. No words of compassion or encouragement. No one spoke or called out, groaned, or whimpered. Only the wind creaking in the sail and humming in the rigging, only the water creaming at the bow and gurgling along the hull, made any sound.

One man sat hunched in the stern, his arms wrapped tight around himself, hands clamped beneath his armpits for warmth, the ruby ring he usually wore gone, lost to the sea. He stared out into the darkness, stared almost unblinking towards where England remained safe and unconquered.

For now.

AUTHOR'S NOTE

England had an efficient navy – and very probably did meet the Normans mid-channel, although there is no proof of it. Unfortunately (for the English) if they did fight at sea, they did not make as thorough a job of destruction as in this story.

Part of Duke William's fleet did, however, wash up in tattered array along Normandy's coastline. He did lose many men and vessels, although Norman propaganda claims the fleet fell foul of a storm.

I believe that it was for this reason – that William had been defeated mid-channel in the late summer of 1066 – that Harold made his one mistake. He assumed Normandy was beaten, at least for now; assumed that William would not be coming again that year. He stood the English fyrd (the army) down and sent the men, gathered along the south coast, home to bring in the harvest.

His one error. He underestimated Duke William's determination and ability.

The Duke commandeered every ship possible, regrouped, and sailed again in September 1066. One of the first men he had captured after his victory seven miles inland from Hastings, was Eadric the Steersman, the English Fleet Commander. He was imprisoned and never saw his freedom again.

With the re-issue of this 2021 edition I did consider changing the ending of this story. I would *so* have enjoyed drowning William... But then, my original intention had been to have him suffer the dep humiliation of defeat and the contempt of his peers. So I left him to drown, in a different sense, by leaving the ending untouched.

One final note, I named the English command ship *Dolphin*, to honour the author, Rosemary Sutcliff. Her superb stories set many a young (and older!) reader on the path to loving the thrill of historical fiction, or to writing our own stories. My greatest treasure is a hand written letter from her, complete with her famous signature of a dolphin. Thank you Rosemary.

Helen Hollick
www.helenhollick.net

DISCUSSION SUGGESTIONS

The English were known to be good sailors (many were of 'Viking' stock), and had a fleet. The Norman chronicles make no mention of it, however. Was this Norman propaganda, stifling the truth? Is it likely that Harold would not have used his ships and his experienced seafarers?

The Norman's were also of 'Viking' stock – 'Norman' derives from 'Northman', but unlike the English, they had become a land-based fighting-machine. Should Duke William have waited, built a more reliable fleet? As it happened, he managed to cross the Channel in September, but what if the wind had not changed? What if he'd had to wait for many weeks or months? Would he have held his armies together?

SEPTEMBER

1066

*S*t-Valery-sur-Somme was a strong place to muster a fleet. The fields around were flat enough to accommodate a large war camp and fertile enough to offer grazing for the all-important cavalry horses. Just as importantly, the estuary was long and wide with plenty of room to keep ships at anchor in relative shelter from the winds – the wrong winds. For William might be ready to set sail for England, but the winds were resolutely against him (although they were in exactly the right direction to speed the Viking ships to York).

William was trapped on his own shores with a huge army to provision – something he had sworn to do without ravaging a single estate in the area – and with what must have been a growing feeling amongst the ranks that God, like the wind, was against the Normans. He must have been frustrated and impatient and he was certainly vulnerable...

THE DANICH CRUTCH
Anna Belfrage

For almost twenty-four years since Edward became King in the early 1040s, England had been at peace (discounting minor squabbles and the matter of Wales.) His reign was relatively prosperous because of it. The building of abbeys and churches took precedence over fortified defences – which is why there were no stone-built castles in England prior to 1066. The political upheaval caused by the death of Edward not having an heir, however, spread further than just Normandy. Whatever happened in England could affect trade for all the countries that bordered the North Sea – and beyond.

Sven Estridsen, King of Denmark, would be one most affected, for he was related to Harold Godwinson, and relied on various trade agreements. If William of Normandy were to conquer England, all that could change – and not for the better...

There was scaffolding everywhere – round the church that was slowly growing out of the ground, round the royal manor house a stone's throw away. The tip-tapping of chisels on stone, the sound of hammers on nails, of men yelling in foreign tongues. Gunhild Ingvarsdotter kept even pace with her father, who now and then stopped to greet a man, slipping effortlessly from one language to the other.

'Whatever else, one can't fault Sven Estridsen's eye for location,' Ingvar said with a wry smile. Gunhild nodded. Built on a small bluff, both church and manor had unimpeded views to the west, the fields a rippling sea of golden, ripening barley, the copses of oak and beech rustling in the wind. Somewhere beyond the bustling town of Lund was the sea, and someday Gunhild hoped to travel even further west – to England, where her father had been born, or even to Paris.

'Hmph!' Mother said. 'This is your land, and just because he's eager to arse-lick every churchman that comes his way, it shouldn't be you being forced to give it up.' She sniffed. 'Prime land, at that.'

Ingvar shrugged. 'He gave me a fair price.' But he didn't like it, Gunhild knew, especially as Ingvar was expected to contribute in kind to the building of Sven Estridsen's new church.

'Fair price?' Mother's voice rose. 'You should have bargained for more! Leif says—'

'Leif? Who cares what he says?'

Off they went on one of their interminable arguments, and Gunhild fell back, wincing at her mother's piercing voice. Hallgerdur was a forceful woman, equipped with a sharp tongue and hard hands. Rarely did she emerge the loser from any of her quarrels with her husband, so it rankled that in the case of the land here at Dalby, Ingvar had ignored her and done as the king asked.

'Yet another church to the White Christ,' Hallgerdur yelled. 'This land is the land of Oden the wise, not of that milksop of a God who allowed himself to be sacrificed!' She cut quite the figure, wearing her best red wool over her linen shift decorated with her silver jewellery, brooches set with precious stones fastening her tunic and cloak. Silver chains criss-crossed her chest, there was silver on her wrists and on her fingers.

Ingvar caught hold of her. 'Keep your voice down!'

'Why?' She pulled free. 'I am not afraid to say what I think!'

'Unfortunately,' Ingvar muttered. Hallgerdur launched herself into yet another vitriolic attack, spouting one insult after the other. Anger made her extraordinarily beautiful, cheeks flushed a vivid pink, eyes flashing. Like Leif, Gunhild thought sourly, just as her half-brother stepped into sight.

Leif was ten years older than she was, and as tall, as fair, as mean-tempered as Hallgerdur. They did not share a father, something Ingvar often said was a blessing, as who knew what mischief Leif was capable of when he'd stared too deep into a mead-horn or two. A lot, Gunhild suspected.

'Mother!' Leif raised his hand in a wave, and Hallgerdur went from angered harridan to simpering mother in a heartbeat. Gunhild shared a look with her father who rolled his eyes. With Leif came Magnus Gunnarsen, and Gunhild groaned: not him again, not this persistent suitor the size of an ox who was also Leif's boon companion. She clutched at the amulet round her neck depicting Thor's hammer while mumbling a few lines of the *Pater Noster* – she did that a lot, hedging her bets by invoking both the gods of old and the new god – and begged them to spare her from ever becoming this man's wife.

'You don't want him, he'll not have you,' Ingvar murmured in her ear. Want him? She'd rather die in a peat bog than lie beneath that mountain of a man! Unfortunately, Hallgerdur was an eager proponent of the match – anything to please dear Leif – and sooner or later, Ingvar would cave.

'Ingvar!' A booming voice carried over the building site. 'Come to inspect my efforts?'

'Don't see you wielding a chisel,' Ingvar shot back, and the man laughed, picking his way towards them. At his back came a couple of armed housecarls, and from the way people bowed and scraped, Gunhild deduced this was Sven Estridsen himself. He was accompanied by a fair youth and tall dark-haired man with a crutch. For an instant, the cripple looked at Gunhild, eyes as dark as forest tarns met hers, and Gunhild's chest squeezed together, making it impossible to breathe.

'It is good to see you,' Sven Estridsen said once he was standing before Ingvar.

'And you.'

They shared an embrace, and after some back-thumping the king released Ingvar and turned to nod first at Hallgerdur, then at Gunhild.

'She looks like Inga. A spitting image of her aunt.' Sven smiled at Gunhild. 'If you are anything like Inga in character, the man who weds you will be a fortunate man.'

'Me,' Magnus said from behind Gunhild. He set a hand to her shoulder. 'I aim to wed her.'

Gunhild shrugged off his hand. 'I will not have you.'

There was a sharp tug on her braid. 'Leave that to your betters,' Leif snapped, before bowing a greeting to the king. 'Leif Hallgerdursen, at your service.'

'Hallgerdursen? You don't have a father?' Sven Estridsen looked him up and down.

'I do, but he is insignificant.' Leif straightened up to his imposing size. 'Just like you, I take greater pride in my mother.'

'Ah.' Sven Estridsen shot the young man beside him an amused look. 'Tell me, Knut, will you also adopt your mother's name rather than mine?'

'No.' Knut grinned, shoving his thick fair hair out of his face. 'Knut Svensson, that's me, and I'm proud of it.'

Gunhild suppressed a little giggle. Leif was looking from one to the other with a confused expression.

'And just so you know, I take as much pride in my father, the great jarl Ulf, as I do in my mother. But Estrid was the daughter of a king, granddaughter to Harald Bluetooth. Her name ties me to a line of kings and queens. What does your mother's name tie you to? Outlawed pagan practices?'

Hallgerdur went a bright red. 'Our gods—'

'Do not exist,' Sven interrupted. 'And anyone who says differently, I'll have nailed to the church door – by their ears.'

Hallgerdur paled and licked her lips.

• • •

'Oden's eye,' Ingvar muttered as he followed Sven towards the manor. 'Did you have to be so brutal?'

'I'll not have it. This…' Sven swept out his hands. '…is a Christian kingdom. We embrace learning and light, not blood-sacrifices and superstitions. So best make your wife see that – quickly.'

'It's not easy to make her see anything she doesn't want to see,' Ingvar said.

Sven curbed the desire to say something scathing. In his house, he ruled, and his women would never question his authority. But all he did was nod, leading the way to his hall.

'Is your daughter as good at handling her blade as her aunt was?' he asked over his shoulder.

Ingvar grinned. 'Better, I'd say.'

'And does she have your gift for languages as well?' Sven reduced his pace to allow Rolf to keep up. Recently crippled, Rolf still had days when he struggled with his crutch – although today it seemed to be the fair Gunhild who caused him to lag, Rolf's gaze affixed to her slender shape.

'She does. Speaks the language of the Franks like a native, as well as English.' Ingvar preened. 'And she knows her prayers in Latin.'

'Don't we all,' Sven muttered. In a louder voice, he added; 'She'll make that Magnus a good wife.' He led the way into the shadowed interior of his hall.

'You heard her. She doesn't want him, and I fully understand why. A vicious streak a mile wide, which is probably why he and Leif get along so well.' Ingvar frowned. 'Leif owes Magnus gold – a lot of gold. I wouldn't put it past him to use his sister as payment.'

'What?' Knut said. 'He'd sell his sister?'

Ingvar squirmed. 'More like place her in his bed and oblige her to wed him afterwards.'

'And you'd let him?' Sven asked, wondering what had happened to Ingvar's balls.

'Not if I knew about it beforehand. But Leif is a wily fellow, and Hallgerdur worships the ground he walks on, so—'

'Send her away.' Rolf leaned heavily against his crutch. 'A pretty girl with an aptitude for languages and sharp blades has many uses.'

'Maybe so.' Sven gave Rolf a sharp look. 'Could you use her?'

'If she's willing.' With a grunt, Rolf sat down in the chair Knut offered him. Knut squeezed his shoulder, no more. Best friends since the cradle, and now, due to that stupid accident, Rolf could no longer keep up. It made Rolf bitter and angry, complaining loudly that he was so useless he might just as well throw himself over a cliff. Which was why, of course, Sven had offered him a new venture.

'Use her for what?' Ingvar asked. At Sven's invitation, he joined them at the table.

'What do you know of what is happening out in the world?' Sven asked.

'Not much. Well, I heard Edward of England died – not much of a loss, if you ask me – and that Gytha's son has claimed the crown.' Ingvar grinned at Sven. 'Your baby cousin, king of England, and here you are, mouldering in Denmark.'

'Let's see how long he keeps it.' Sven poured them all some ale.

'Keep it?' Ingvar asked.

'Harold is a fine man,' Knut said. 'But the kingdom he rules is a quagmire of treachery and deceit – starting with that brother of his.'

'Ah. Tostig.' Ingvar sipped at his ale.

'That one has the wits of a fly in a honeypot,' Knut said, making Sven smile. Tostig was hungry for power, for glory, but he was no fool – or maybe he was, seeing as he'd run all the way to Harald Hardrada to demand help in ousting his brother from the English throne. Sven tightened his hold on his cup.

'Tostig is in Norway,' he said, 'and Harald Hardrada is preparing to invade England and claim the throne for himself.'

'No!' Ingvar sat back. 'Insatiable bastard, isn't he?'

Sven gave him a grim look. Harald had defeated Sven on a number of occasions, and where once Denmark and Norway had had one king, now they had two, Harald ruling Norway while Sven had to make do with Denmark. It rankled – God, how it rankled. He cleared his throat.

'I'd hate it if that Norwegian idiot placed his hairy arse on the English throne!'

Knut grinned. 'When did you see Harald's arse?'

'When he mooned me at the battle of Nissan,' Sven retorted. 'Anyway, whatever Harald is planning to do, he'll do. Stopping him is like dragging the sun out of the sky – impossible. Besides, it's not Harald that worries me the most. Should he win – and God spare us that, he'd never let us hear the end of it – England would still have a king of Viking blood. It is William of Normandy who is the real threat. For months, he's been howling to anyone who cares to listen that he's the rightful English king, no matter that the Witan has acclaimed Harold. I'll bet my balls William has every intention of grabbing by force what he considers to be his.'

'And can he?' Ingvar asked.

'Don't underestimate the bastard. And if William wins, woe betide our brothers in England. He'll bring his own men across, and the lands of the ancient Danelaw will be soaked in blood. And as to Harold...' Sven slid a finger across his throat.

'So what will you do?' Ingvar asked. 'And how would my Gunhild be involved?'

Sven sat back. 'I want to send her to Normandy – with Rolf here.'

'As spies?'

'As whatever is needed to stop William's invasion from happening.'

Ingvar coughed, spraying the table with ale. 'What?'

'You heard: whatever it takes. Someone has to stop him. He grabs England and any hopes of a strong Danish-English alliance dies. Our trade, our people, will suffer...' Sven gnawed his lip. 'Those Normans are a rapacious lot.'

'Sounds just like us,' Knut offered cheerfully.

Ingvar waved him silent. 'You expect a seventeen-year-old girl and a cripple to stop someone as determined as William the Bastard?'

Rolf leaned forward, something flashed, and Ingvar's sleeve was tethered to the table by a very thin, very sharp blade.

'Never underestimate a cripple,' Rolf hissed.

'Or a woman,' Sven added with a grin. He sighed. 'I know it's a bit desperate, but William is a suspicious man. I can't exactly send Knut here – or other hale and hearty men. But a lame man who sings for his supper and a young girl who accompanies him? William will, just like you, scoff at the thought they may be dangerous.'

'Hmm.' Ingvar pursed his mouth. 'She'll have to decide for herself.'

Sven nodded. 'Of course. Fetch her.'

'What, now?'

'Why put off until tomorrow that which can be done today?' Sven said. 'Besides, we leave within the hour.'

A fortnight later, the overloaded *knarr* they were travelling on nosed its way into the harbour of Saint-Valery. France. Gunhild hugged herself. She'd leapt at the opportunity to leave home. No more Magnus, no more Leif, no more having her skin bruised by his punishing fingers. Come to think of it, no more Hallgerdur, and Gunhild felt a twinge of pity for her father, left on his own against those two. Instead, adventure beckoned and although her innards cramped at the thought of what lay ahead, she would never get another opportunity to see the world. And then there was Rolf, with those dark eyes of his marking him as very different from the men she usually met.

'Will we be going to Paris?' Gunhild asked Rolf, sitting as close to him as she dared. He was not always the easiest of companions, taking out on others the frustration caused by his damaged leg.

Rolf finished chewing his bread before replying. 'Paris? Whatever for? This is where William has his ships, not somewhere up the Seine.'

'Oh.' She was disappointed. The little town spread out before them was dominated by two large round towers to the east, a squat church tower in its centre. A far cry from the imagined glories of Paris.

'They've made a mess of things, haven't they?' Rolf gestured at the various ships that thronged the bay. New ships, for the most part, and yet several of them were under repair, the damage indicating they'd crashed into each other. 'Seems these Normans have forgotten their ancient sea-faring skills.' He chuckled. 'Not that they'll be going anywhere unless the wind turns.'

Gunhild squinted at the clear August sky and stuck up a finger: still a steady westerly wind. They'd been rowing for the last week, with Gunhild and Rolf taking their turns at the heavy oars.

When they disembarked, Rolf went first, crutch under one arm, his precious harp in an oilcloth bag slung over his shoulder. One bundle in his free hand, and he still managed the gangway on his own, waving away Gunhild's offer to help.

She hurried after him, her belongings in one hand, the

other resting on the hilt of the dagger her father had given her. Rolf slid her a look, his mouth quirking into a little smile.

'Good to see you have my back.' He studied her blade with evident interest. 'Where did you get that?'

'It's from Spain. And I don't think you need anyone to have your back.' She pointed at his crutch. 'I daresay you're quite deadly with that.'

'I am. People see someone with a limp, and they believe they can help themselves to whatever I have.'

'Let them try.' She moved closer. 'Now there are two of us.'

'Two?' He smiled again – a miracle, almost: two smiles on the same day. 'Woe betide Duke William.'

Gunhild followed him as he limped towards the town, biting back on the desire to help him negotiate the steep and slippery slope from the harbour. A proud man – a handsome man, assuming you looked more than once. After a quick glance at his crutch, very few did, and Gunhild could see in Rolf's stance and set face that it hurt to be so dismissed. She moved closer to him, ignoring the pull of the shops, horizontal shutters standing wide open to display everything from cheese to the finest of silks. Cobbled streets, so many houses – Gunhild's braids bounced as she turned this way and that.

'This is nothing,' Rolf said. 'Compared to Constantinople, this is at most a dung pile.'

'Miklagård,' she breathed. 'You've been there?'

'Several times – my mother hails from there.' He tugged gently at her braid. 'One would think you've never seen a town before.'

'Not like this. Lund doesn't compare.'

'Lund?' He snorted. 'Three streets and a crossroad at most.'

'And a church.'

'Ah, yes.' There was a twinkle in his dark eyes. 'We must not forget the church.'

They made their way down a winding street parallel to the waterfront.

'Where are we going?' she asked, staring at the encroaching buildings, the narrow alleys that led off the main thoroughfare. She'd get lost in less than a heartbeat here!

Rolf hopped over an overflowing and stinking gutter, regained his balance, and lifted his crutch to point at the looming towers. 'There.'

Gunhild came to a stop. For a long, long time she studied the walls, the towers and the heavy gates.

'That William, he lives there?' she asked in a hushed voice.

'Sometimes.'

'Thor's balls!' she exclaimed, her cheeks heating when he raised a brow. 'I just meant…' She sidled closer. 'How on earth are we to stop a man so powerful he lives like that?' She gestured at the castle. 'And look at all his men!'

'Who said it would be easy?' Rolf led the way up towards the main gate. 'And no one has tasked us with tearing down the castle – just the man.'

Gunhild gave him a long look but chose not to comment.

The men manning the castle gate waved them through, no more than a cursory glance at Rolf – a cripple elicited little interest – a far more curious gleam in their eyes as they studied Gunhild. She disliked being scrutinised by unknown men, and moved closer to Rolf. He took her hand, a warm, comforting hold.

They entered the crowded, sun-lit bailey. Here too were shops and tradesmen, the promising smell of warm bread mixing with that of horses and red-hot iron. A smith, an armourer, a fletcher – men trading in weapons rather than fripperies.

Other than the sturdy hall, the enclosed space contained a chapel and an assortment of timbered buildings hugging the walls. There were men everywhere, many of them men-at-arms, even more servants, rushing back and forth across the courtyard.

'There must be more people here than in all of Lund,' Gunhild said, liking that he had still not relinquished her hand.

'Probably.' He slid her a look. 'Not saying much, is it?'

The sound of a horn filled the air and the ground shook under approaching horses. The gateway filled with riders, with horses that snorted and threw with their heads. In the lead rode a man dressed in garments of vivid blue. He drew his stallion to a halt and dismounted fluidly.

'Is that William?' Gunhild whispered. The man looked as impregnable as the castle, broader by far than Rolf, albeit that he was half a head shorter. Rolf nodded, no more.

The duke dragged a hand through his short hair, brows pulled together in a ferocious scowl as he berated the stable-boy for not being quick enough, the damned wind for remaining stubbornly from the west.

'God's will,' one of his companions said, and William turned on him.

'God's will, Odo? Truly? If so, my dear lord bishop, you'd best spend your days on your knees and beseech Him to change his mind – soon!' He made for the ornate door leading to the hall, his companions at his heels.

'It might help if you added your voice to the prayers,' Odo said.

'Damn it!' William kicked a dog out of his way. 'And you don't think I do? Every waking moment I pray – for the wind to change, for me to bring that traitorous, foresworn English earl to his knees.'

'That's the spirit,' Bishop Odo said with a grin. 'I'm sure God will be pleased by your fervour – and piety.'

For an instant, William looked at the bishop as if he

wanted to stake him. And then his features cracked into a broad smile. 'I leave the pious stuff to you and Matilda. I am far better at the fervour.'

'Who's Matilda?' Gunhild asked.

'His wife.' Rolf grinned. 'She has him well-tamed, they say.'

Gunhild snorted. 'Whoever suggests that man is tame is a fool.' She lowered her voice. 'How do we stop him?'

'I have no idea – yet.' Rolf shifted his shoulders. 'I am sure we'll come up with something.'

Four weeks later, and the Normans had repaired most of their ships. William had taken up permanent residence in the castle, his men lived in camps on the outskirts of the little town, and the air reeked of open latrine pits and smoky fires. But no matter the constant prayers of the monks at the nearby abbey, no matter how often William strode back and forth along the shoreline staring out across the sea, the westerly wind prevailed.

'Good thing,' Gunhild said as they made for the hall and the evening meal. 'Seeing as we still don't know how to stop him.'

'You could always lure him with your feminine wiles and then I could swoop in and kill him.'

'Me?' Gunhild squeaked.

'He has noticed you.' Rolf sounded gruff. 'No wonder, seeing as you sit beside me every night as I sing, all that hair of yours unbound.'

Gunhild's hands fluttered up to her hair. 'Should I braid it?' After years in Hallgerdur's shadow, she enjoyed the novelty of being gawked at, men commenting on her fair hair, her blue eyes.

'Leave it. You look beautiful.' He took her hand, and she smiled inside at how his fingers tightened round hers. 'I truly don't know what Sven expected us to achieve.' He sounded tired. 'The only good thing is that there are plenty of others here with the same ambition we have – to thwart his invasion.'

'There are?'

'I've seen at least twelve Saxon spies. The French king must have a handful here as does the King of the Germans. Truth be told, it's a miracle the duke is still alive, what with all these well-wishers. But then, William has ample practice in avoiding assassins. They started coming after him when he was but a child.'

'Assassins? I'm not sure that is something I want to be.'

'We may not have a choice.' Rolf gnawed his lip. 'The best thing would be to sink his ships, but he has more guards posted on his precious vessels than a pig has bristles.'

'A distraction,' Gunhild suggested. 'A big distraction.'

'Yes.' Rolf turned towards the stables. 'That might do it. A blaze threatening the horses, and while everyone is busy here, those ships can be dealt with.'

'How would that work? You can't move fast enough to...' she choked off the rest.

'No.' He adjusted his crutch. 'The cripple can't rush for the ships, but the cripple can light a fire.'

'I didn't mean it like that – and I've never called you a cripple.'

'That's what I am, isn't it?' he said bitterly. 'Useless and invisible.'

Gunhild tightened her grip on his hand. 'Not to me.'

'No?' His eyes met hers.

'Never.' She held his gaze.

At long last, he cleared his throat. 'I think we need to talk to our Saxon friends.'

'Took some time to bring them aboard,' Gunhild said some days later, her belly heaving with apprehension. This was it. She licked her lips, glanced at Rolf. A girl and a cripple – God help them!

'The thing about spies is that they don't like admitting to being spies,' Rolf replied, guiding her across the bailey. Night was falling fast, and down by the main entrance the guards were shooing people out of the castle before shutting the gate for the night.

'No wonder. Duke William finds out and he'll…' Gunhild mimed a closing noose around her neck.

'Aye.' Rolf cut her off, nodding a discreet greeting to Wulfric, a Saxon disguised as a monk who rushed for the gate, making for the harbour and his hidden comrades. Everything was ready. 'After tonight it is over.'

Gunhild wiped her hands on her skirts. 'May we both see tomorrow.'

'Amen to that.'

She grasped the silver hammer that hung around her neck. 'Thor guide us.'

Once the castle had settled down for the night, they rose from their hiding place in the stables. In absolute silence, they went along the walls, lighting candles at even intervals. Round each candle a heap of straw and rags dipped in oil.

They emerged from the stable, moving from one shadow to the other. When they reached the armoury, Gunhild spread her cloak to shield the flame Rolf ignited, blowing on it carefully until the bundle of rags in his hand caught fire. They threw it atop the heavy thatch, and soon enough the roof began to glow.

Rolf took her hand and led her towards the dark hall.

They were waiting just beside the entrance, when the shout went up.

'Fire!' someone yelled, and the roof of the armoury burst into flames, huge red things that licked the wall behind it.

The sentries at the entrance set off at a run, and Rolf moved fast, pulling Gunhild with him. In through the door, and he pressed her into a nook just as several men came thumping down the passage.

From the courtyard came loud orders, men yelling for water, for the gate to be opened. A horse neighed. Another shrieked in return, hooves crashed into walls, more frantic neighs. The stables were now on fire as well.

'Go!' Rolf whispered to Gunhild, and she hastened down the passage, screaming that the castle was on fire, and God help them all. Half-dressed men spilled from the hall, running for the door and the conflagration beyond.

'Christ on his cross!' someone exclaimed. 'The horses, we must get them out.'

She came to a halt by the duke's chamber. The door was flung open, two young men in nothing but their shirts rushing by her.

'Fire!' she screamed, clutching at the duke as he made as if to follow his men. 'God's judgement is upon us! This is His punishment!'

'Shut up!' Duke William shoved at her.

Gunhild clung to him. 'God has seen your greed, my lord!'

His hands closed on her shoulders. 'This is not God's wrath, you fool, this is…' He sniffed. '…You! This is you!' His hands slid up her neck. 'You smell of oil and smoke. Why, you treacherous wench, I'm going to…' His hold tightened. Gunhild gargled. No air. She tried to scratch his face, kick at him, helpless as he strangled her. A shadow loomed behind him. The crutch went up, it came down. With a sickening crunch, it connected with William's head. He toppled to the floor. Rolf swung again, and blood and other matter spattered her skirts.

'Thor and Christ save us!' Out, they had to get out! Gunhild scuttled down the narrow passage, Rolf at her heels. Men, coming the other way, calling for the duke, and Gunhild's mouth was dry as tinder.

The courtyard was in chaos: panicked horses, men with

buckets, smoke and fire. It hurt to inhale, the air stank of singed hair and roasting flesh, and the cobbles were slippery with water. Over by the gate, horses were milling about, surrounded by men who were trying to calm them down sufficiently to lead them across the narrow drawbridge.

'We must…' Gunhild said, just as someone screamed that the duke was dead.

'There!' a man yelled. 'Catch the cripple and the girl!'

'Run.' Rolf pushed at her. 'Flee.'

Gunhild grabbed hold of his hand. 'Not without you.' They hastened towards the gate, weaving a path between restless horses and shouting men.

'Close the gate!' someone yelled. 'Stop them!'

Rolf cursed and increased his pace. Already, two of the sentries were trying to close the gate, but the horses neighed and bucked, kicked and jostled.

'This way!' Wulfric appeared beside them. In among the horses, and Gunhild held on to Rolf's belt, terrified of these huge animals. An arrow whirred by, and Gunhild yelped.

'Down!' Wulfric yelled, and they were crawling on their hands and knees, making for the rapidly closing gate. 'Faster!' Wulfric hauled Rolf along. 'Move, man!' Gunhild slid outside, caught hold of Rolf's hand and pulled. Wulfric tumbled after, and they were through, just as the gate banged shut.

'Dearest God,' Wulfric gasped, leading them down a narrow alley. 'That was close.'

'Not over yet.' Rolf spoke through gritted teeth, hopping as fast as he could.

'They have other matters to handle.' Wulfric grinned and pointed to the bay, where smoke and flames billowed upwards. 'Like their burning ships.'

'And their dead duke,' Rolf said.

'Dead? God be praised!' Wulfric raised a fist heavenwards.

'Or Thor,' Gunhild added in an undertone. It was over. Tremors flew up her legs, her arms, and she staggered against a wall.

'Gunhild?' Rolf pulled her into a brief embrace, his lips pressing into her hair. 'It is done.'

'Done,' she repeated. When he held out his hand, and she took it, following him into the protective darkness of the September night.

AUTHOR'S NOTE

When Edward the Confessor died many countries in Europe held their breath. The succession in England was an uncertain thing, with William of Normandy vociferously putting forward his own claim. In Denmark, Sven Estridsen kept his fingers crossed for his cousin Harold Godwinson – not only because blood is thicker than water, but also because Denmark and England had commercial interests in common. This is also why Sven, in 1069, joined forces with Edgar Atheling in an attempt to dislodge William. However, after capturing York Sven was bought-off by William and left Edgar to his fate. In 1074, Sven launched yet another invasion force, but by then William had consolidated his hold over England, and the attempt failed.

Sven was one of the first Danish kings to genuinely embrace the Christian faith. He had a personal relationship with Adam of Bremen and was one of the more enthusiastic church builders. The church of Dalby was begun around 1065 and carries the distinction of being one of the oldest stone churches in Sweden (although at the time, Dalby was in Denmark).

I have named my female lead Gunhild because of an apocryphal story about Sven: reputedly, Sven married a certain Gunhild, daughter of his Swedish foster father, Anund Jacob. The church was mightily upset by this union, and Sven was obliged to divorce his wife who went on to found a convent instead.

Why the church would have been upset by this marriage is unclear – until the full story emerges, as per which there were two Gunhilds involved. The first was Anund Jacob's daughter, but she died very soon after the wedding, then Sven took as his wedded wife Gunhild's mother – also a Gunhild. This was what had the church in knots, this is why Adam of Bremen forced Sven to divorce his wife, threatening him with eternal hellfire unless he complied. Sven did as asked, but never married again, no matter that he fathered well over twenty children.

And as to Hallgerdur, may I recommend you read Njals Saga to meet her fire-breathing namesake?

Anna Belfrage
www.annabelfrage.com

DISCUSSION SUGGESTIONS

How influential were the 'old gods' at this time? Do you think only a few, or many people, like Gunhild, hedged their bets between old and new religion?

With no modern artificial aids, how did disabled people manage? How much difference would there have been if you had a disability and you were either rich or poor?

OCTOBER

1066

*1*066 is the most well known date in English history, for on that fateful 14th day of October King Harold of England fought Duke William of Normandy on Hastings field and, in the dying light of an almost unprecedentedly long battle, lost. It was, perhaps, an especially tragic defeat coming off the back of Harold's amazing victory over Harald Hardrada at Stamford Bridge, almost three hundred miles north, just three weeks before.

Details of the Battle of Hastings were reported in various accounts, all of questionable accuracy, and debate will always rage over whether William was unhorsed and believed dead, whether he ordered a 'feigned retreat' to tempt the English out of their shield-wall, and whether Harold died from an arrow in the eye – which for various reasons is now considered unlikely.

It matters little. Although William was not yet a king at the end of that bloody day, he had started his campaign in the most brutally successful way possible. Not only King Harold but many of his key lords lay dead and William was well on the way to taking the English throne.

Resistance, however, would be strong and as a result, the Battle of Hastings effectively ushered in several years of rebellion and bloodshed, culminating in the vicious 'harrying of the north' that saw whole villages laid waste. Such violence, beyond the key battle itself, may not have been William's original intention but he was a man used to rebellion, having fought endless challenges to the title of Duke that he'd inherited aged only seven, and he was merciless in putting them down.

So many more lives were lost to William's victory than those taken on the field in October, and it will forever be tempting to imagine a world in which it had been William, not Harold, who lay cut to pieces at the end of that famous 'Battle of Hastings' – actually fought atop a steep-hilled field seven miles from the small harbour town...

HOLD ENGLAND FIRM
Joanna Courtney

If you've ever had the luck to go to the Battle of Hastings re-enactment at Battle Abbey, you will have heard, as I have, the vast majority of the spectators vigorously boo-ing Duke William. Most of us still, despite so much of our heritage coming from our Norman ancestors, believe in our hearts that Harold was the just and good English defender and that William was the vicious foreign invader.

Certainly at the time, King Harold was desperate to see William from his shores. This was the man who had forced him, under duress, to swear an oath of allegiance. This was the man trying to steal England on some trumped-up promise no one else remembered. And this was the man who was ravaging his own patriarchal lands around Hastings. Harold had beaten Hardrada in a surprise attack and he was keen to do the same to William. He rode out from Westminster before his northern reinforcements had caught him up – a rare impetuousness that may well have cost him the Battle of Hastings. If only he had waited one more day...

I was not born to be a king. I know that without others pointing it out. I did not even ask to be a king. I was chosen, and chosen for one reason only – my ability as a commander. I am not here on England's throne for my bloodline, or my heritage, or my links to other royal houses. I am not here as part of any grand scheme; I am here to defend my country. I am here to keep the invaders from our shores.

I am half way there. Already we have seen off the Vikings. Even now, Hardrada's body will be on a ship back to Norway, wept over by his queen. I am sorry for it, for I hear tell he was a great ruler but this is war. If it had not been him going to God it would have been me and I am not ready to die. I have a job to complete and tomorrow, on the fifteenth day of the October month, I will complete it. Together with my men, I will hold England firm.

The English camp stretched out as far as the eye could see, swamping the ancient moot point of the now wizened hoary apple tree. And still men came. Even now, Harold could see a new group coming out of the thick trees of the Andreaswald – maybe fifty of them, led by a squire who was barely bearded and riding on a packhorse that looked as if it might expire at any moment.

His men had an eclectic collection of weapons: rusting swords with only their new-cut edges shining in the low autumn sun; knives of all sizes, no doubt taken from the kitchen or the threshing barn; and hoes and spades and rakes that might have looked comical save for the fierce determination with which they were wielded. These men had come with all they had to fight for England and Harold rushed to welcome them to his army. He would have felt safer, perhaps, had they been in chainmail with fine new blades, but raw courage counted for much in a shield wall and he grabbed keenly for their hands.

'Welcome, welcome. Thank you for joining us.'

The men, wide-eyed, dropped to their knees at the sight of the crown on Harold's head.

'King Harold, my lord. We are honoured indeed.'

'No please.' Harold rushed to raise them. 'It is I who will be honoured to fight at your side tomorrow. England will need all her sons to keep the Normans out.'

This elicited a roar of approval and Harold seized the chance to move away, adjusting the heavy crown as he went. He felt a little foolish wearing it in the rough war camp but his brother, Garth, had insisted that the men needed to see him as a king and he was right. These new recruits would fight harder for having stood before their ruler. If Harold was to be a king, he was determined to be a good king and if that started with jewels on his brow, so be it.

It will make you an easy target, a voice inside his head reminded him but he paid it little heed. He had led armies for years with his 'fighting man' standard high over his head and had not yet been cut down. His chainmail was of the finest quality, his helmet of the thickest steel and his sword sharpened to cut bone like butter.

The royal swordsmith had done the sharpening in London, saying Harold could not ride on the Normans with Viking guts dulling his blade. There was time, he'd insisted, and everyone had said the same. The Normans were going nowhere. They'd set up one of their ridiculous little wooden castles at Pevensey and were happy hiding within its walls. Harold, they'd all said, could take a few days to regroup and recruit and rest.

'Rest?' he'd roared at them. 'How can I rest with scum on our doorstep? In my own earldom? How can I rest whilst they raid my villages to feed their greedy troops and cut down my trees to make arrows for our hearts?'

Everyone had looked scared at that, even Garth. Harold had been a little loud, perhaps –there must be traces of his father in his blood after all, God bless him. Born the son of a lowly thegn, Godwin had fought his way up to become England's topmost earl and had passed that honour to his eldest living son, Harold. How proud he would have been now, to see his son as king.

Harold pushed his chin up at the memory of his father, the crown no longer so heavy on his head, and went to find his commanders. He was calmer than he'd been in London. It was a relief to be here on the brink of battle. He just wanted it done now, wanted the bastard duke dead and his ravening troops gone from England. He'd have been here yesterday if he could have but Edyth had stopped him.

'You want me to rest I suppose?' he'd snarled at his queen – yes, snarled. Perhaps, on reflection, he *had* needed rest.

'No,' she'd said crisply, 'not if you don't want to, but I do need to talk to you.'

She'd been very calm, very certain. Amidst the clamour of soldiers and battle plans, her clear voice had spoken out to him.

'Very well,' he'd agreed. 'Here?'

'In our chamber.'

The men had bellowed approval at that, coarse lot that they were, but Edyth had just smiled. Having been Queen of Wales for nine years she was well used to coarseness.

'I wish,' she'd said, loud enough for all to hear, 'to give my king something to fight for.'

They'd liked that, the men, had clapped lustily as she'd led him away by the hand, he the one blushing. He'd known Edyth from a young girl and been married to her nearly nine months but still she surprised him with her strength and resourcefulness. Without her and her two brothers, Edwin and Morcar, the lords of Mercia and Northumbria, he could never have held the North.

It was Edyth who had been forced to entertain Hardrada at York after his victory at Fulford; Edyth who had delayed the delivery of the hostages until Harold could get his army there; and Edyth who had kept the citizens of York silent as they had marched through to surprise Hardrada at Stamford Bridge. He had married her for her northern connections and it had paid off, but now she'd given him even more.

'I am with child, Harold,' she'd told him that day in Westminster.

He'd gaped like a fool.

'With child?'

She'd smiled then.

'Yes. It is not, you know, that much of a surprise. I have three children already by Griffin, do I not? And you five of your own, and we have, you know, created plenty of opportunity.'

He'd blushed again like some virgin boy and not a man on his second wife, though she'd spoken true. He had married her for political convenience but the match had been no hardship in the bedchamber, though bedding her had been different from with Svana, his handfast wife of twenty years. It had been harder, faster, more tangled with the fierce world they had been thrown into on Edward's death, but they had both embraced it along with their other duties and now this.

They'd lain side by side the night she'd told him, talking it over for hours. Their son would unite the north and the south for good, they had sworn to each other. England would be whole and stronger for it. They'd spoken of Wales too. Griffin was dead but Edyth's two sons, Ewan and Morgan, carried his blood and maybe, in time, could be restored to the throne of Wales, forging bonds with England's neighbour where previously there had been only strife. Such plans they'd dreamed up – and they would make them work too, once the Norman was defeated.

'Garth, Leo!'

Harold found his brothers eating stew outside their pavilion with all his other key lords and housecarls. They were in their armour already, though spies had reported that William was camped beneath the trees to the south of Caldbec hill. Battle would be joined in the morning and by this time tomorrow it would surely, be over? Harold looked to the skies, purpling with the first colours of dusk, and prayed he would see the sun set again, for if he did not it would mean he had failed and England had fallen. But that would not happen.

'Any news of our northern troops?' he asked, glancing back into the Andreaswald through which the dusty road led up to London.

'Yes, Sire,' Garth said using the new French term coming into fashion among the noble kings of Rome.

Harold grimaced at him.

'Call me, Harold, Brother, please.'

'Yes Harold – *Sire.*'

Garth winked at him and Harold had to smile. His brother was irrepressible. He would have to find him a wife and settle him down once the battle was won.

'Where are they?' he asked eagerly.

'Barely half an hour away, my King. They will be with us before sunset and with two thousand men at their backs.'

Harold looked again to the skies, now turning orange as the sun sank with a sigh of a breeze over the great sloping field on which tomorrow they would play out England's fate. He sent a prayer of thanks up to God above and thought, again, of Edyth. He had slept after her news – slept deep and long. Too long, or so he'd thought. He'd risen the next day furious at himself but then word had come that Edwin and Morcar, recovered from Fulford – or at least recovered enough – were already at Bedford and moving fast to join their king against the Normans. And now they were almost arrived with just enough time to rest before the most important battle of any of their lives.

God was good. It was the fourteenth day of October and tomorrow, the fifteenth, they would stand side by side – Northerner and Southerner alike – to England's defence.

Men do not like to defend. It is hard to sustain. It requires patience, determination, control. Defending does not sing through the blood as attacking does. To stand and take another man's repeated charges requires a stubborn stamina that can grind a man down. And yet that is what we must do – at least until the time is ripe to break.

We cannot fight cavalry in the open field. I know, for I fought with William in Brittany two years back and have seen, first hand, the havoc an armed rider can wreak upon foot soldiers. I have seen too, though, how fast horses tire in battle, how easily even the most fiercely trained beast will rear from a well-placed spear. No horse will charge a wall, even a shield wall, if it is well made and well held. And a Saxon shield wall is always well held.

William will not take us. I will not allow it. Maybe I was not born a king but I was, at least, born an Englishman. William has no more right to the throne than I. He claims he was promised it but such promises are ever made and broken and only a fool boy holds to them in this reckless way. He is not wanted here. Does not every rake-armed soldier prove that, especially those who have marched from York still fresh from victory over the Viking? All of England stands here with me now and all of England will stand here with me at the conclusion. Together we will hold England firm.

They lined up at dawn, though men had been stirring long before. Few sleep well in the face of battle. It matters little for the pulse of battle-lust keeps the heart beating and the mind sharp and there will always be plenty of time to rest afterwards, one way or another. They'd left the camp in the hands of the old men and the followers – the myriad women weaving between the soldiers, feeding their stomachs and, often, their more carnal appetites. Imminent mortality can be very arousing but now the fires were burnt low and the women left behind to rest and prepare to receive the inevitable wounded once battle was joined.

Harold's own wife and queen had ridden in last night, high in the saddle at her noble brothers' side.

'What are you doing here?' Harold had demanded.

'I ride with the men of the North to your aid,' had been the proud reply.

'And what am I to do with you now?'

Much laughter but in front of the common soldiers Edyth had been all dignity.

'I shall ride to Whatlington to await news of your victory in safety.'

'You have a guard?'

'Of course, and a companion besides.'

She'd pulled her horse aside and there, to Harold's utter astonishment, had been Svana. His wives had been friends for years when he had been wed only to Svana but his second marriage had, needless to say, driven something of a wedge between them. Seeing them there, together, had brought home to him how truly all of England was united behind him and he had nearly, God save him, wept.

Garth had rescued him, leaping forward to pump the hands of Edwin and Morcar and welcome them at huge volume, to their camp. The men had cheered so loudly at this huge boost to their numbers, that Harold had sworn William must have heard them on the far side of the valley. The thought had set steel in him again. Let him hear; and let him quake. They were coming for him.

And now, here they were. The Normans were coming

out of the trees and lining up and, Lord, there were a lot of them. The legendary cavalry were at the back, horses frisking, long lances glinting, pennants flapping cockily in the breeze. In front of them were lines of infantry, many of them mercenaries from all over northern France, and all with armour and weapons. No rakes for the Normans. And then, in front of them, were row upon row of archers. He would have to watch them. The wall would need to keep shields high overhead. Instinctively Harold pushed down on his own helmet but it was secure. He wore no crown today, merely a simple diadem studded with jewels, sitting over the rim of his helmet.

'Like a halo,' Garth had joked this morning as they'd checked each other's mail before leaving camp.

'Saint Harold!' Leo had laughed.

'I'm no saint,' Harold had shot back, tense. 'How can I be when I killed our brother?'

But at that Garth had grabbed him by both arms, holding him hard in his warrior's grasp.

'Tostig deserved to die, Harold. He fought against you, up there in the North alongside Hardrada – he fought against England. You had no choice.'

'It's true,' Leo had agreed, serious now. 'Though true, too, that you're no saint. You have two wives, man!'

Harold had forced a smile.

'We will get you wives, both of you. You will be heroes once today is done.'

'Heroes,' Garth had agreed happily. 'And how much better is that than saints?'

Now Harold looked over to his younger brothers, stood with his other commanders awaiting his final orders. Leo and Garth had revelled in being safely down the family line, both living the free lives of warriors, and despite being over their thirtieth year now, were wild yet. They were earls, though and, more importantly, were brave men and true. They would lead well today if they could keep their heads.

'We must hold the wall,' Harold said urgently, striding over to them. 'It may take all day but we must hold the wall until the moment is ripe.'

'How will we know when that is?' Leo demanded, looking eagerly to the Normans below.

'I will sound the horn – five long blasts. But it will not be quick, Leo. You must hold.'

'You said.'

'It is important,' put in another voice and Harold turned to see Edwin of Mercia.

His brother-in-law was very young, just two and twenty years, but Fulford had hardened him. He'd been on a losing side that day and had to flee for his life – Harold could see in his eyes that he had no intention of ever doing so again.

'Look at the slope,' Edwin went on, pointing to the fresh sheep-grazed field rolling down from their feet to the enemy. 'That will tire their men and their horses but it will take time. I swear we will have to stand for the full curve of the day before we can take them.'

They all looked to the sun, rising low over the east side of the field and casting a falsely pretty light over the two great runs of soldiers on either side. Harold traced its path in his mind's eye, seeing it pass over as quickly as if it were the fire-tailed star from Eastertime. He gritted his teeth.

'To arms, men! We hold until five blasts sound and then – then we will smash them back into the Narrow Sea.'

Those nearest roared their approval and the sound spread out all along the several-deep lines as Leo and Garth, Edwin and Morcar, and all the lords moved to head up their troops. Leo was on the left wing, Garth the right, with Harold dead centre, and Edwin and Morcar commanding the sections either side of him. Harold sent up another prayer of thanks that the Northern lords had made it to his side. They knew of Edyth's pregnancy too now and the babe joined them to Harold even more tightly than before, making them so very valuable as his allies.

Had he gone to battle even one day earlier, his ranks would not have been half so deep, nor his command half so steady. Putting back his head, he blew a single blast on the horn and as one the men of the front line took a step forward and their shields clunked into place as surely as if there was mortar between them.

'*Ut!*' came the call: Out! The ancient Saxon battle cry. '*Ut! Ut! Ut!*'

Below, the Norman archers fell to their knees and cocked their crossbows.

'*Ut!*' the men roared louder. '*'Ut! Ut! Ut!*'

And battle commenced.

Harold had known it would be tough – had he not told his commanders as much – but even so, the day seemed to grind out like a millstone over corn. Every time the Normans mounted an attack the men braced themselves, and every time they backed off to regroup Harold could feel the whole shield wall quivering to follow and knew that resisting the urge was every bit as tough as resisting the charges.

The trained soldiers were used to it, from Harold's own elite housecarls down to the appointed militia-men, drilled at least occasionally in the art of the shield wall. For the brave men who had come straight from the harvest, however, set on seeing the invaders off their shores, just standing and taking a hammering went very much against the grain.

And then, as the sun reached its apex, sending sweat down all collars, be they chainmail, waxed leather, or simple wool, there was a crisis on the left flank. A cavalry charge led by Duke William himself met fierce resistance that sent the horses into disarray. In the scramble several men were unhorsed and suddenly a cry went up: 'The duke is dead.'

Harold felt it thrill through him. Could it be? Certainly the Norman lords looked panicked – several were already riding back to their ranks as if preparing to flee.

'Can you see?' Harold asked those in front of him. 'Can you see what has happened?'

But this far along the field no one could for sure and now, with a roar, part-rage, part triumph, Leo's men were breaking out of the wall and charging into the tangle of Normans.

'Hold the wall!' Harold bellowed on instinct. 'Hold the wall!'

Out of the corner of his eye he saw Morcar stopping the rush and was grateful, but even so he strained as hopefully forward as the rest of his men, praying for this to be it, the end, before too many precious lives were lost. But someone was riding out from the melee, helmet lifted high, head bared and Harold saw, as everyone did – Saxon and Norman alike –Duke William shouting encouragement to his men. Not dead but alive – alive and with Leo in his sights.

'No!'

The cry choked from Harold and he looked for Garth far out on the right as the Normans, with renewed courage and purpose, circled in on the loose Saxons and their lord and cut them swiftly and systematically to the ground. Harold did not see his brother die, but felt it in his soul – a sharp, bitter, crushing blow that almost felled him for a moment. Planting his feet in the churned up soil of Hastings field, he seized the pain and rolled it up inside him into a red-hot ball of fury. He would see William gone from here. Leo, God bless him, had been too hasty. They must wait. They *would* wait. But then – then they would strike.

The day ground on. Harold left his central troops with his ablest housecarls and trod all along the line, encouraging the men and re-affirming their strategy with the commanders. Already it was clear that the horses were weakening. The day was still warm and the slope was hard work for them, especially now it was littered with bodies and slick with blood. The Norman crossbowmen had arrows yet but there were more sticking uselessly in Saxon shields and Harold was sure the invaders must be losing heart. If it was hard to stand and wait for attack, how much harder was it to attack again and again for no apparent reward? The Northern reinforcements had easily plugged the gap left by Leo's tragic charge and there was no way through the solid defence along the ridge. Norman heads were dropping; they were surely losing heart.

Harold looked up. The sun was on its way downward now, already dipping towards the trees in the west as if it, too, was worn out of this fifteenth day of October. When Harold looked back he saw that the Normans had paused and could see their comrades huddled around their duke.

'Hold the wall!' he cried for what must be the one thousandth time. 'They are breaking,' he added. 'Hold it and our time will come.'

The men roared back, the sound frayed at the edges but determined yet. Harold smiled. It felt strange amongst the blood and the fear but these men, these Englishmen, were his and he was so, so proud to have been chosen as their king – chosen for this; for battle. They needed him and he would not let them down.

He squared his bulky shoulders. They were stiff and sore but he cared not. Not much longer. He watched intently as a new charge formed, led this time by the Bretons on the Norman left, distinguishable by their black and white pennants and their stout ponies, smaller than the Norman horses – smaller and more manoeuvrable.

A memory flashed through Harold's tired mind – '64. He'd ridden on campaign into Brittany with Duke William. He'd been 'invited' to it after the duke had released him from capture by the Count of Ponthieu, leaving Harold in his debt. That had been before William had tricked him into swearing to uphold him as king. That oath, made on holy relics – though Harold had not known it until after – had tortured Harold when Edward had neared his end. He'd even considered supporting William but the Witan had refused to countenance it for a moment. They'd wanted an Englishman as king and Harold had had to respect that – as he had to uphold it now.

He focused on the Breton ponies as they lumbered up the slope and, remembering them in a similar situation near Dol two years ago, suddenly he knew exactly what they were going to do.

'Garth!'

His brother did not hear him at first, but Earl Edwin did and roared the cry on over the battle shouts of the men. Garth looked round and his gaze locked with Harold's. Harold knew not if his brother heard his next words but prayed his lips had formed them clearly enough for Garth to understand: 'Feigned retreat.'

He said it over and over and suddenly Garth's eyes narrowed. He gave a curt nod and turned urgently back to his men. Harold saw heads turn as an order rippled along the shield wall and watched nervously as the Bretons pulled back suddenly and fled. The Normans jeered convincingly at them but not convincingly enough. The Saxon shield wall shook but held and only the shadows of the dead chased the Bretons back down the hill.

Harold's gaze swung back to William and he saw it – panic in every part of the duke's tense body. Even his horse was prancing, its coat lathered in the white sweated foam of fear. Harold took a deep breath. It was time. Lifting his horn to the fading rays of the sun, he blew five long, deep blasts.

The Englishmen surged down the hill like dogs released from the leash, salivating for a bite at the enemy who had tormented them all day long. The Normans, still caught watching the uselessly fleeing Bretons, were helpless before them. The tide of Saxons – Northerners and Southerners both – ripped through their ranks cutting down men and horses as the dark, pulsing cry of 'Ut, ut, UT,' sounded like a drumbeat over the wails of dying Normans. Harold ran with them, sword aloft, cutting out vengeance for Leo, and for England.

And now the Normans were turning to flee. Their ranks were decimated. Dead strewed the ground and the mercenaries who had filled their ranks for money alone had already fled, back down the long road to their ships at Pevensey. Harold cut and thrust with the rest until the field was all-but bare of standing Normans, and suddenly there he was – William.

He was on his knees in the bloody field, his horse dead, surrounded by Harold's housecarls, the last of his lords with him. Harold stood still. Everything seemed to fade – the death-cries of those still pursued by his farmer's army, the whinnies of panicked horses on the loose, the whistle of swords slicing through the last of the light. He drew in a long, deep breath.

'William the Bastard' he said coldly.

Duke William of Normandy looked up at Harold, his eyes white with fury and hatred.

'Harold Oath-breaker,' he answered with a defiant sneer.

Harold nodded slowly. So, there was to be no plea for mercy, no offer of negotiation or treaty. He considered the options – if he let William limp back to Normandy would it ensure his gratitude and allegiance, or would it simply leave England exposed to future attack? Would pardoning him look strong or weak to the eyes of others? For himself, he did not want this man on God's earth one day longer, but was execution here, or after legal judgement, the correct way forward?

He looked down at his bloodied sword. What was the point of hollow words after all that had passed today? There were men dead on this field because of the greed of one man. Mothers had lost sons, wives had lost husbands, daughters had lost fathers and brothers. Now, above all, was the time to stand up and be King to his people.

Calmly Harold lifted his sword and placed the tip against William's throat, between the straps of his helmet and the linen padding of his chain mail hauberk. He looked into the invader's eyes, unblinking, then in one swift motion he thrust his weight against the blade, hearing the crunch as it pushed through his enemy's gullet. William's body crumpled at his feet and his blood splattered across the legs of his cowering lords like brutal flowers.

Harold stood a moment, his hands clasped on the hilt, then let the sword go, took a step backwards and crossed himself as he looked up to God. The Sun was all but gone and the light was low and run through with red – too much red. There had been enough slaughter.

Slowly Harold bent, removed the sword with a twisted jerk, and lifted William's body into his arms. He nodded one of the remaining Norman lords forward.

'You – take your duke home. Show him to his sons as a warning never to tread upon English shores again, then give him honourable burial. He was a worthy duke, but he was no king. Today God has proved that and we thank Him for it.'

The Normans nodded, bowed and, taking what was left of their duke, scuttled away after the last of their ragged troops. Harold watched them go then turned back to his own, brave men with a bitter smile. There had been too many dead this day, but they had won and pray God this would be the last of it.

· · ·

I was not born to be a king but I was chosen one – chosen by those wise in experience and backed by people I am proud to represent. I was crowned on January 6th 1066 but did not truly take the throne as my own until October 15th, the day of our great victory at Hastings. That day I stood side by side with my fellow Englishmen and faced down a great threat to our dear land. And that day I learned what they already knew – how precious this land is to us and how eternally grateful I will be to God for blessing us with his love in victory.

The people sing my praises now. It embarrasses me, save that in praising me, their king, they praise themselves. And now Edyth has birthed me a son – a second Harold – to follow in my path, a boy who is truly born to be a king. Praise God and all my countrymen that at Hastings we fought hard, we fought together and we held England firm.

AUTHOR'S NOTE

When I found out that I was getting to write the alternative Battle of Hastings I couldn't believe my luck! I'd found it heartbreaking writing the ending of my novel *The Chosen Queen* in which Harold, my hero, was hacked to death barely an hour before the reinforcements who could have saved him arrived. Writing this story was, therefore, cathartic to say the least.

And this version was so, so possible. The Battle of Hastings, from what we can gather, started around 9 a.m and Harold was not killed until sometime around 4 p.m. That's a long time for a medieval battle – normally one or two hour affairs at most – and it being October it was almost dark when he was dealt his deathblow. What's more, the northern troops do seem to have been very close and it may well have been them who lured a large number of Normans to their death in the 'malfosse' behind English lines after the battle was over. If the shield wall had only held firm for another hour, both sides would have been forced to retreat and rejoin the next morning, by which time Harold's numbers would have been swollen and victory far more likely.

One of the mysteries of October 1066 is why Harold marched south to meet William quite as quickly as he did. William had built a castle at Hastings, and he was pillaging the area, but he was quite well contained on the peninsula and showing no signs of marching north. The sensible option for Harold when he reached London after his long march from Stamford Bridge would have been to wait at least another few days to rest his troops and allow more to join him. So why did he not?

He may have sought to emulate the surprise attack he'd mounted so successfully on Hardrada. He may have been incensed at the attacks on his own people as the heart of his patriarchal lands were around Hastings. Or perhaps William had decided to move position, realising, as Harold would have done, that it would be folly to be caught, trapped, in that narrow peninsula of land. Once out on to the expanse of the Weald, it would have been hard for Harold to stop him. Or, Harold may just have been driven mad with the desire to have William gone and all the fighting done with. He was a man, after all, who had been through much since being crowned on January 6th. Whatever the reason, his haste to go into battle with William may well have cost him the victory and that is what I wanted to explore in this story.

Joanna Courtney
www.joannacourtney.com

DISCUSSION SUGGESTIONS

What good did the Normans bring to England? Much of what we consider to be 'Olde' English – the St George style crusading knight – came to us after 1066 so if Duke William had been defeated, would we have had that at all? Would we have bypassed chivalry? How long would we have continued to live in wooden halls instead of stone castles? What, in all this, is truly 'English'?

Was Harold truly revered as a monarch, or just needed as a war-leader? If he had defeated William at Hastings, how long might he have lasted as King? Would that victory have secured his place on the throne (and that of his baby son, Harold, after him) or would he still have been under threat from Edgar, who was of royal blood and rapidly coming of age?

NOVEMBER

1066

*D*espite his victory at Hastings, William was not yet King of England. He seems to have waited at the battlefield for some time (even, reportedly, eating his dinner amongst the carnage) perhaps hoping to receive a full surrender, but that never came. Indeed, another had been named king in his place.

Edgar 'Aetheling' (meaning 'throneworthy') had come to England in 1057 with his father, Edward the Exile who was the royal son of Edmund Ironside, son of King Aethelred, and had been in exile since he'd been smuggled away from the conquering Cnut as a baby back in 1016 (exactly one thousand years ago in this year of 2016!) Sadly Edward had died within days of reaching England, leaving Edgar, his only son, as the 'true' royal heir. In 1066, however, he was only about thirteen which was why Harold, a proven leader of men, had been elected to the throne in his stead. Now though, with Harold dead, the remaining lords hastily proclaimed Edgar as king. To take the throne Duke William was going to have to take London.

William adopted a policy more than familiar to him from years of putting down rebellions in Normandy – tracing a circuitous line to London, raiding and pillaging everywhere he went. This was designed to have the double effect of feeding and enriching his own men, and of aggravating his enemy and it worked. Dover and Canterbury both surrendered, as did Winchester, but London, with its high walls and one fortress-like bridge across the Thames, and Westminster, secure on Thorney Island further along the Thames, were harder nuts to crack...

THE BATTLE OF LONDON BRIDGE
G.K. Holloway

Although Edgar had the strongest claim to the throne, when in January 1066 the Witan had to elect a successor to Edward, they chose Harold Godwinson, a proven commander and a respected Earl. After Harold's death on the battlefield, England needed a new king; the young Edgar was the only choice. If things had worked out differently for him he might well have enjoyed his coronation on Christmas Day 1066. As it transpired, he spent most of his life rebelling against William and his successors.

Edgar died childless at the age of seventy-five, the last male of the House of Cerdic, the original English royal family. Edgar's sister, Margaret, fared better – she married King Malcolm III of Scotland and their daughter, Edith, married King Henry I of England.

London Bridge – Late November

Inside London's bursting walls, anxious citizens cram the streets, grudgingly sharing their town with the newcomers – the vanquished soldiers from the battlefield and refugees fleeing atrocities. Throughout the thoroughfares rumours of gruesome massacres, merciless maiming, butchery and barbarism at the hands of the Normans are spreading like the plague. People are asking questions of each other. *What was it like at Stamford Bridge? What was it like at Hastings?*

Where are you from? Why did they burn it down? And the question, *'Is the same fate in store for us?'* hangs on everyone's lips.

With similar thoughts running through his mind, Edgar Edwardson, the sixteen-year-old King of England, stares out of his chamber window in the Royal Palace of Westminster. His gaze follows along the stretch of cold, grey river to the City of London, shrouded in dread. The last leaves have fallen from the trees and only black, skeletal branches appear against the skyline.

Over the horizon, Duke William of Normandy and his army are heading remorselessly towards them, swarming over the countryside, destroying everything in their path. He will arrive within hours but the mighty Thames should offer protection from the fury of the Normans. As long as the English can hold the single bridge leading into London the city will be safe. Edgar shivers and pulls his cloak tighter to keep out the cold.

The Witangemot, the Great Council, proclaimed Edgar as king only a few weeks ago. His coronation, yet to take place, is set for Christmas Day. Most of his subjects see him as their only hope but he knows there are others who have an alternative ruler in mind. The northern earls, Edwin and Morcar, have made sure that their sister is safe, hundreds of miles away in the city of Chester where they hope she will give birth to a healthy boy, the late King Harold's son.

King Edgar is well aware of the unreliability and lack of fighting prowess of the earls. The brothers are not fearless warriors, but their men are sorely needed. Their sister, Queen Aldytha, has done the right thing in fleeing London. But now people are asking the question - if they can't even protect their sister, who can they protect?

Staring out of the window, King Edgar hopes to find inspiration for the task ahead. True, there are soldiers at his disposal but they are demoralised and he is untried as their leader. Earl Waltheof's housecarls tasted glory at the Battle of Stamford Bridge but they are just two hundred in number – will they be able to have a decisive impact in the forthcoming clash?

The rest of the trained troops number several hundred more but they are the remnants of Harold's men, lost souls with spirits shattered by defeat. Who cannot pity them? After all, did they not lose the biggest battle in England's history? And worse still, failed to defend their former king. Can they now successfully defend their new one to set themselves up for future winter nights at the fireside, recounting tales of a glorious victory?

Edgar is sure that none of them relishes the thought of fighting for an inexperienced youth. He has heard the mutterings – if Harold, the victor of Stamford Bridge, lost to Duke William, what chance does a mere lad stand? He has heard them and, worse, he fears they are right.

Edgar knows the fate of the kingdom hangs on this next battle. His heart pounding, he heads for the great hall to make plans with his commanders – the three remaining earls and his senior housecarl, Bondi Wynstanson. Tall, blond and muscular, his long hair hanging halfway down his back and a mutton-chop moustache any Saxon would admire, Bondi has a strong presence and he is unswervingly loyal. It is easy to see why King Harold held him in such high esteem.

All the men have their war gear close to hand; swords and a couple of big battle axes lean against the wall of the great hall. Edgar too has his own sword and a hand axe, useful for close combat and for throwing. Both were inherited from his grandfather, the legendary Edmund Ironside. Still not able to grow any real facial hair, Edgar wonders if he has the right to carry such weapons.

'How did you take Stamford Bridge?' he asks Bondi, wishing he'd been there.

'By surprise,' Bondi answers laconically, adding, 'the

Vikings had no idea where we were until we attacked them.'

'Well, we know when the Normans will be here, so that's one advantage they won't have. What is our situation now?'

'We have a full body of men guarding London Bridge. They may not be many but their position is strong; they can stop an army.'

'They will have to.'

'Trust me,' says Bondi, 'Duke William does not see us as real opposition and that works in our favour.'

'With so few troops, is it possible?'

'We have to trap him somewhere where we have him at our mercy, and that will be on the bridge.'

'Yes. It is our only hope.'

There is a knock on the door and a servant enters, bows low.

'There is a messenger here who wishes to speak with Earls Edwin and Morcar.'

'Show him in.'

The messenger creeps in, bowing low to Edgar, but when he eventually speaks it is the northern brothers he addresses:

'Lady Aldytha sends word that she has given birth to a son.'

Edgar sees both Edwin and Morcar's eyes light up as they register that they are now

uncles to the late King Harold's heir. They have never, he thinks bitterly, shown an interest in any of Aldytha's other children but, then, her other children are not the sons of a king, albeit a dead one. This is no ordinary child and Edgar is as aware of this as his earls. Sitting silently on the dais, he observes them in animated conversation, happy to accept the congratulations of Bondi and Waltheof and his fears are confirmed.

'Join us in a toast, my lord,' says Edwin with a broad grin.

As the small party raise their drinking horns, Edgar realises that he always thinks of Edwin and Morcar as though they are one. The brothers always act together and are twice as strong for it. In fact, they hold the strongest position in the country, yet they appear to have little interest in using it for the general good and Edgar is the first to realise Duke William may now not be his only cause for concern. Who knows what those two might get up to?

But that is a concern for the future. For now the northern earls are as trapped as he, for the only thing standing between Duke William and the crown is Edgar and his tiny, battered army. He stands decisively – he is England's elected leader and must act like one, however afraid he feels inside.

'Waltheof, what do you think? Can we hold the bridge?'

Waltheof is only in his twenties, but has already proved himself in battle.

'If we hold the bridge, then we hold the city, I am certain.'

'Good.'

'But that is not enough, my lord.'

'What do you mean, not enough?'

'We have to do more than that to stop this Norman upstart. If we do not, he will cross upriver and fall on the city from the north where our defences are weak.'

Edgar eyes Waltheof closely.

'What do you have in mind?'

'We have to do to them what they did to us. We have to remove the head from the body – we have to kill Duke William. None of the rest of them has a claim to the crown. Remove William and we remove the threat. Then they will go home.'

Bondi nods slow agreement. Even Edwin and Morcar look convinced.

'You speak true, Waltheof,' says Edgar.

They will have to find a way to rid themselves of William permanently. And soon.

As darkness falls, Duke William, flanked by a few of his closest comrades, arrives with his army at deserted Southwark on the south bank of the Thames, opposite the walled city of London. The Duke, a powerful-looking man, sits astride his horse appraising the scene. Burned-out houses and farms are all he can see on this side of the Thames. The locals have already crossed the river looking for protection inside the city walls and they have taken their possessions with them. What they could not take, they have destroyed.

William looks across the river to where he can see the warm glow of lights in London. He is disappointed that the city has not surrendered to him - though he keeps his thoughts carefully from his ice blue eyes. No one knows what William is thinking – he makes sure of that.

'My lord,' a scout calls, riding up out of the half-light, 'the bridge is blocked. The Saxons are manning a barricade on the far side.'

'Never mind,' the Duke replies in his gruff voice. 'We will cross it in the morning. By this time tomorrow we will be supping beer in Westminster Palace. At first light, we will storm the bridge. Tonight we sleep in tents but tomorrow we will be staying in the finest accommodation England has to offer!'

Next day, the dawn breaks to reveal the first hoar frost of the year. All round a cold, thick fog rises up from the Thames, obscuring the far bank. The long bridge, shrouded in mist, vanishes into a grey void, heading toward the unknown. His back firmly to it, William addresses his commanders, Sir William Warenne and Sir William Fitz Osbern:

'My lords, first we will parley with the English. We will tell them we understand their desire to defend London. We will say that if they surrender now then no harm will come to them or their city, but if they put up a fight we will make them suffer.'

The knights nod in approval but although they are brave, none of them are keen to cross the river. The sight before them looks like the entrance to the afterlife. Stretching out into the void is a rickety looking bridge made of rough-hewn planks supported on oak trestles. To prevent travellers falling into the river a railing runs along each side. William de Warenne eyes the mist-shrouded bridge curiously.

'My lord, I wonder, should we not take Sir Hugh with us?' he says eventually.

'Why would we want to take anybody else with us, William?' the Duke asks.

'Because when we arrive on the other side of the river, the four of us will appear out of nowhere,' he replies, with a roguish grin. 'We will look like the Four Horsemen of the Apocalypse – and add a little spice to their English fear.'

'Very well,' says William, also grinning, 'we will take Hugh.'

Sir Hugh Grandmesnil joins his comrades and the fearsome looking four begin to make their way slowly through the greyness on to the bridge. Their horses' hooves thud on the wood as they walk toward their enemy. As they cross the river, they feel the temperature drop, chilling them to the bone. The horses clop over the bridge, the sound of their hooves echoing the drip of the cold, moist air on the water below. Each man is trying hard not to shiver so that when they make their dramatic arrival, they do not look as though they are trembling with fear.

'My friends, how do you think the English will react

when they see us emerging from this fog like spectres?' Sir William Warenne says.

'They'll probably run for their lives,' replies Fitz Osbern.

'If they haven't run away already,' quips Warenne.

The group progress steadily, as though they know that no matter how slowly they travel, the outcome will be the same; Edgar will submit. There is no doubt, no need to hurry and they continue taking their time, prolonging the anticipation; hoping the slowness of their advance will allow dread to fill English hearts. But as they make their approach they can barely see each other and their own hearts are far from steady.

As they reach the far side of the bridge, the Duke makes out the barricade looming up through the gloom. It is a makeshift affair of wagons, broken furniture, old barrels and even sheaves of straw; primitive but effective. Five feet in height, it makes a formidable obstacle and the Duke assesses the grim and anxious faces of the defenders behind its protection.

Amongst them, he sees someone he takes to be Edgar, standing beneath a blue and gold banner, which hangs limp in the still air. The young man is wearing a full chain mail coat but it is his distinctive helmet with a brightly gleaming gold boar crest that singles him out. William recognises some of the thanes and notices a resolute young nobleman who he believes must be Earl Waltheof. He looks for Edwin and Morcar and sees them standing determinedly behind their king. He almost laughs at the youth of these so-called English leaders. These young men, he gauges, will give him no trouble.

As the English are all on foot, they have to look up to the horsemen and, having succeeded in intimidating them, the Duke's men are enjoying their advantage. Warenne produces the finest of arrogant sneers and Hugh encourages his stallion to rear, shod hooves sharp above English heads.

From amongst the defending army, the fresh-faced Edgar calls out. 'Duke William, what is the purpose of your visit?'

'That's King William to you!'

The Saxon housecarls greet the comment with a roar of abuse, which takes a while to subside. William Warenne, who speaks very little English, only gets the gist of the conversation but he is pleased to see the defenders are upset. When things quieten, Edgar speaks again.

'Let me remind you, it is I who am the rightful King of England and that is why I and not you wear the crown. If you, Duke William, want this meeting to proceed, you need to recognise that. Now, what is your question?'

'My question is, does your mother know you are here?'

Edgar swallows the insult and thrusts back as hard.

'My Lady Mother dressed me in my armour and handed me my Grandfather's sword! Have you merely come to insult me? Have you naught better to do this day?'

'I have much to do but I thought while I'm here, I might as well poke at the beardless boy I see before me.'

'I think you had better leave, sir, while you still can.'

'And I think you had better submit to the rightful King of England and save a lot of bloodshed.'

'*I* am the rightful King,' Edgar replies slowly, as though to a simpleton.

'We will see about that,' says the Duke menacingly.

'Yes, we will,' Edgar agrees.

As they turn their horses to leave, Warenne looks King Edgar in the eye and runs a finger across his throat, grinning wickedly all the time. It makes a fearsome sight but Edgar reacts well, laughing as though at a mischievous child.

'Look,' he says, 'he is cutting his own throat!'

His response is appreciated by the defenders and the Normans kick their horses into a canter to escape the jeers, grateful now for the safety of the fog.

'Tell me, what do you think of them?' asks the Duke of his commanders as they ride back over the bridge.

'Edgar is too young and too inexperienced to command a robust defence,' Warenne says. 'The others are not much older. I think they lack the stomach for a real fight.'

William is boosted by this opinion.

'You are right. There was more lost at Hastings than Harold Godwinson's life. England's lost its head and its heart. Prepare the infantry. Once the barricade has been breached, the wretches will panic and run, then England will be ours.'

Fitz Osbern organises the men. William's plan is for the infantry to breach the barricade by sheer weight of numbers, after which they will charge through the streets of London with the cavalry. The infantry lines up shoulder to shoulder, packed in as tightly as herrings in a barrel, and the Normans advance. Crossbowmen line the banks of the river to either side of the bridge, while the defenders chant the familiar Saxon war cry: '*Out! Out! Out!*'

The river is shrouded in wraiths of fog as the Duke's men advance, grey shadows in the thick mist. The muffled thud of their Norman feet is a comfort as they march forward into dank, grey oblivion. On the bridge the English also hear the approaching *thud, thud, thud* of footsteps but can see nothing. Only the sound of the advancing army escapes the murk. As at Hastings, the English continue their rhythmical smashing of weapon against shield to drown out the sound of the ominous footfall.

Guessing his enemy is now in range of his Saxon archers, lined along the northern banks, Edgar gives the command to shoot. Those who had failed to complete the journey from the north in time to be of use at Hastings, now make their presence felt. The Normans swarming across the wooden bridge hear Edgar's command – hear but do not understand the English words until arrows rain down on them.

The English archers may not be able to see their targets but they know the bridge and know where they must be. There are soon many fatalities amongst the Normans. In the sightless haze, disembodied cries are heard all around as men, pierced by arrows, fall screaming to the rough-hewn wooden planks or over the rails into the cold, unforgiving water below. A wounded man, lying unseen and bleeding, is no longer a soldier but an obstacle over which a comrade might trip or stumble. He is ignored, trampled, crushed by the boots of the men pressing ahead across the bridge.

Edgar continues to bellow commands: 'Keep shooting! Keep the pressure up. Even if you can't see a target. We've more than enough arrows to complete this task!'

Whoosh follows *whoosh* as hundreds of arrows soar through the damp air and then a clatter as they land on shield and armour, and a softer sound like a sigh when they find flesh. Visible only when too late, appearing from nowhere, they mow the Norman soldiers down. The grim reaper moves amongst them like a phantom harvesting his gruesome crop but determined, the Normans continue to advance and at last they reach the far side.

Emerging from the murk Warenne catches sight of Edgar standing with his housecarls behind the formidable barricade.

'Forward! Forward!' he cries, then intrepid as always, he forces his own way forward.

Inspired by his courage, his infantrymen push on harder under the hail of missiles. They can see the dark figures, fearsome spectres ahead. Spears fly towards them out of the cold, dim haze to strike soldiers down but still the Duke's men stay resolute and advance until they reach the makeshift defence. Using their shields for cover, they push with all their might in an attempt to force the obstacle aside.

Now they are so close to their foe they find spearmen jabbing at their faces and others standing on carts and huge barrels, throwing hand axes down on them. More and more of the infantrymen fall wounded or dying and warm blood seeps between the wooden planks of the bridge to mingle with the icy river and the bodies floating below.

Along the south riverbank, the Norman crossbowmen are having little impact. They are at the limit of their range, have no view of their targets in the fog and are hampered by their own men along the bridge. On the northern shore, however, the English archers continue to let fly their arrows at their attackers. The English blockade is yielding to the weight and press of men, but not enough, too slowly, and at too high a price. Duke William decides the losses are too great to continue.

'Pull back!' he cries above the din. 'Pull back!' No one hears him. 'Pull back!' he yells, louder.

The order is echoed by his commanders and the withdrawal gets under way. Duke William can see from his soldiers' relieved expressions he has made the right decision.

'*Out! Out! Out!*'

Insults and calls of derision follow them as they retreat across the bridge, stumbling over fallen comrades. On the south bank they appear as bloodied apparitions before those who have remained behind.

'My lord,' Fitz Osbern says quietly to Duke William, 'I think we need a change of tactics.'

'Indeed,' responds the Duke sarcastically.

He eyes the wounded. A couple of hundred injured soldiers have made it back but he thinks there may be as many as seventy or eighty lying dead on the bridge.

'My lord,' says Fitz Osbern, 'we can succeed but not yet, not while this fog is working to their advantage. Their arrows can reach our vanguard but our crossbowmen cannot touch them. When it lifts, that's when we can storm the bridge. We can make a battering ram, break into the barricade and charge through, they'll be unable to repel us. If we rush them with enough infantry we can do it.'

'What kind of a battering ram?'

'We will make one from a tree trunk and a cart.'

'And push it across the bridge?'

'Exactly so, my lord.'

'You'll need to clear the bodies.'

'I'm sure I can get Edgar to agree to that, my lord.'

'Good. It's agreed,' says the Duke. 'We will clear the bridge of the fallen, wait for the fog to lift, and then we will take London once and for all.'

The previous evening, they had thought the final victory would fall into their hands as easily as a ripe fruit from a tree, but this particular fruit was not quite ready for the picking. They all knew that after victory there was plundering and that this would be plentiful in London. Not far away, but out of reach, riches await them. Inside, they rage with frustration.

Nearing midday, after Fitz Osbern has claimed the dead and the warmth of the sun has cleared the foggy air, the Norman crossbowmen gain sight of their adversaries. With their greater range they are to pick off as many English archers as they choose.

Fitz Osbern has ordered some of his men to make a battering ram. Soldiers have cut down an oak tree and secured the trunk to a handcart. Now it is ready they wheel it into position at the front of the column.

'Advance!' Fitz Osbern commands.

The men begin pushing the cart forward. Once on the bridge, the soldiers push harder and the cart begins to pick up speed.

'Charge!' the call goes up from the Duke.

'Charge!' call out Fitz Osbern and Warenne.

They do as urged, forcing the cart over the bridge and

halfway through the barricade as the rest of the infantrymen, led by Fitz Osbern, bear down rapidly behind. The fighting is vicious and bloody.

On the riverbank the crossbowmen are shooting furiously.

'Remember,' their sergeant shouts out, 'they can loose their arrows at a fearsome rate but they haven't got the power or the accuracy of our crossbows. Now that we can see, let us show them our worth!'

And they do, shooting at half the rate of the English bowmen but hitting their targets more often. Just as at Hastings, the effect of their accuracy thins out English ranks. They inflict a terrible fear on the defenders but the Saxons remain unyielding.

'Make every bolt count!' Walter shouts.

His waving arms and loud commands make him a target for the English archers on the far side of the river, but for all the arrows that come his way, none strike home.

Edgar is standing in a place that commands a good view of the proceedings. Now that the Normans are tearing down the barricade and swarming over it with renewed vigour, fear strikes into his heart. His inexperience is beginning to show. Defeat looks certain and death seems close. The Norman cavalry are coming on to the bridge, following in the wake of the infantry and drawing close with frightening speed. Edgar stands transfixed – he's never seen the power of cavalry before but the survivors of Hastings all around him are clearly dismayed at the familiar sight. The veteran housecarls look nervously one to the other as the tension mounts and spirits wither.

'Steady men. Stand firm,' Bondi calls out. 'Those horsemen cannot hurt you. They are harmless while they are on the bridge. You can see they are held back by the foot soldiers. Hold steady and all will be well.'

Edgar is glad of Bondi's resolve but his relief is immense when a grinning Waltheof also appears at his side. The blood-spattered earl appears to be enjoying himself.

'Things are looking lively, eh, my lord? Come with me, we will liven them up some more.'

He is buzzing with battle, though behind him Edgar can see Morcar and Edwin losing confidence. He looks to Bondi, who has also caught the dismay on the northern earls' faces.

'My lords,' Bondi urges the brothers, 'let's push forward and we will have the day. We cannot afford defeat. If they take London the rest of England is bound to fall. Your lands with it!'

Edwin and Morcar nod and, with a quick look to each other, visibly gather themselves.

'Forward, men!' they call out and watch as their housecarls press on in attack, repelling the Norman infantry swarming over what remains of the barricade.

'Follow me!' Waltheof commands.

Desperate to kill the enemy, he leaps into the vanguard of the men. Like a demon, he flails his axe this way and that, scything down his enemies. Bodies fall, draping the barricade like sheaves of corn left out to dry as Bondi rushes to join him.

Still the Normans keep coming; nothing seems to deter them. Climbing over corpses as if they were mere logs in a forest, they appear blind to danger and happy to die for their duke. Edgar lifts his grandfather's sword and, taking courage from its heft and history, obliges them.

'*Advance! Advance! Advance!*' Fitz Osbern bellows.

'*Out! Out! Out!*' cry the English in reply.

Axe, spear and sword crash against shield and chainmail. Sometimes the weapons find their way to soft targets – piercing flesh, breaking bones or cutting through limbs. Fallen men are dying, their screams anonymous in the din of battle.

The Normans are willing to make any sacrifice in their relentless pursuit of victory. After all, do they not have the Pope's guarantee of absolution? And the prize lies tantalisingly close – the whole of London waits a few yards away on the other side of the crumpled barrier that is no longer protecting the city or its people. But in its place, are the English, determined to hold firm as a new barricade – a shieldwall of living, breathing, angry warriors.

Inch by bloody inch, the English are being beaten back. Pushing forward heedlessly, more and more of the metal-clad Normans have come across the bridge. There seems no end to these men who are eager to feel the bite of the axe, keen to suffer the slash of the sword, happy to fall on the spear. The vicious attack rages on even though the dead are piled high. Believing victory is close, the Norman infantry fights all the harder, Duke William is there, mounted on his horse, urging them on.

'Forward men, forward! They are weakening. One last drive will do it. Push on. Push on forward!'

The English housecarls can feel the pressure and they fight more fiercely, the fury of the attack defying reason. It is frenzied and it cannot be repelled, but those who fought at Hastings are anxious to make amends for the cruel death of their King Harold.

Edwin and Morcar continue encouraging their men from behind, Bondi, Waltheof and Edgar are leading the defence – Waltheof slaying many with his huge battle-axe, Edgar cutting down his foe with his grandfather's sword. The young king takes heart from his comrades and from deep inside a warrior emerges. Revelling in the glory of battle, he rushes to fight any Norman within reach until he sees his nemesis, the Duke, a few yards away astride his spirited warhorse. There, tantalisingly close, is the man responsible for all this slaughter, barking orders to his frenzied fighters.

His gaze meets that of Duke William. For a moment

they stand frozen, their eyes hard and staring, then William spurs his charger and Edgar leaps forward, each desperate to hack their way through to the opponent whose defeat spells honour and glory for the victor. But the ferocity of the battle keeps the men apart and frustration grips Edgar as, thrusting and slashing with his grandfather's sword, he tries to reach his man. And then he remembers Ironside's other legacy.

Swapping his sword to his left hand, eyeing his quarry, he pulls his throwing axe from his belt and he hurls it as hard as he can towards the Duke. Too late William sees his rival. Too late the Duke raises his shield. Such is the power of Edgar's throw that the axe strikes deep into William's chest renting the links of his chainmail, sending him screaming to the ground. The would-be conqueror is helpless and pain washes over him as he falls.

Quickly his men lift him up and half drag, half carry him to safety. But now there is no leader, the Duke's men fall back, while the English butcher those on the north bank before throwing their bodies into the river. Where otters usually play there is now blood and gore, and the stench of death. It is over – the battle is done and the Saxons are the victors.

With the men cheering him on, Edgar makes his way to the riverbank, seeking out William on the other side. There, in the bright afternoon sunshine, he sees the Duke being carried into his tent. Edgar waves his sword at him and grins. William's sightless eyes see nothing.

'What is the matter? Was our welcome not warm enough for you?' bellows Edgar across the red-tinged water, but the words are drowned out by the chanting of his soldiers.

The English are celebrating their victory against this

foreign foe. Now they think, with relief, that they have a leader in whom they can have faith.

The next morning the Normans are gone, never to return. Taking their Duke for burial in Normandy, they have melted away like yesterday's fog. In London a week-long celebration begins. And, far away in Chester, a newborn baby cries.

AUTHOR'S NOTE

Why did Duke William invade England? He claimed Edward the Confessor had promised him the throne and that Harold, Earl of Wessex, had sworn an oath to support him. When King Edward died, the English Council elected Harold. William, outraged by Harold's audacity, invaded England to take the crown for himself. After Harold was killed at Hastings, William assumed he would be declared King – he was not. Instead Edgar was proclaimed King. He was the grandson of King Edmund Ironside and therefore of royal blood. Duke William had promised his followers land and riches as their reward for helping him overthrow Harold. He could not allow his companions to go empty handed. After Hastings he had no choice but to take the crown or his followers would have turned on him. And so he marched on London and fought a battle at London Bridge, which he failed to win. He then crossed the Thames up river and fell on London from the north. The English surrendered and William's coronation was held on Christmas Day 1066.

His long reign saw troubled times. There were a succession of uprisings that went on for many years, and William was only able to subjugate the English by building stone castles the length and breadth of the kingdom. Previously unseen in England these massive structures were designed to impose awe and fear, to intimidate – and for the Normans' own safety and protection.

What would have happened had the Norman invasion been a failure? The English would have carried on ruling themselves much as before and probably developed in much the same way as the rest of Northwest Europe. Today, the UK might be more like the Scandinavian countries. One thing that is certain, our history would be very different. There may have been none of the wars with the French, no Henry V, no Henry VIII, no Elizabeth and who knows, no British Empire. Then again, perhaps the British Empire might have been even bigger.

G.K. Holloway
www.gkholloway.co.uk

DISCUSSION SUGGESTIONS

Why is London so important? Why didn't William lay London under siege and leave the English holed up there? He could have made Winchester or York his capital instead – why didn't he?

There is a tale that Harold survived Hastings. Badly injured, he fled England and became a hermit monk. Is this likely do you think?

DECEMBER

1066

*H*aving failed to cross into London at Southwark, William marched his troops in a circle of destruction through what are now Surrey, Hampshire and Berkshire until he finally crossed the Thames at Wallingford where Archbishop Stigand of Canterbury surrendered to him. The rest of the cowering lords did so a little later at Berkhamstead, allowing William to finally march into the Royal Palace of Westminster as the acknowledged – if still vastly unpopular – king.

He was crowned on Christmas Day 1066 in the recently built Westminster Abbey, amidst chaos as a roar at the point of crowning led his guards to torch many houses beyond the abbey, scattering the crowds – including those gathered within to witness the coronation – and leaving William to be crowned in haste and almost alone. It was not an auspicious start.

Nonetheless, William was determined to see himself painted in a good light as a just, Christian and, above all else, rightful king. He ordered an abbey built at what is now Battle as penance for the lives lost on Hastings field and he also ordered some impressive PR.

The Bayeux Tapestry, probably commissioned by William's brother, Odo, Bishop of Bayeux and Earl of Kent, set out to tell the story of William's conquest through Norman eyes – starting with Harold's mysterious visit to Normandy in 1064, focusing on his apparent oath to uphold William's claim, and finishing with William's 'noble' victory.

However, the tapestry seems – whether for reasons of skill, spite or just practicality – to have been sewn in England and experts point to the lively and often rather scurrilous images sewn into the borders as an indication that those making it were trying hard to insert their own voice into the heavily political message of the main narrative...

THE NEEDLE CAN MEND
Eliza Redgold

One of the most famous relics of the 11th century is the Bayeux Tapestry. It is called a tapestry, but in fact it is an embroidery. It is nearly 70 metres (230ft) long, and 50 centimetres (20in) in height, and comprises of fifty scenes stitched on linen with coloured woollen yarns

It is kept, now, in a museum near Bayeux Cathedral in Normandy, where Odo, Duke William's half-brother, was bishop. Some say it was Odo who commanded the Tapestry made, perhaps it was, perhaps it wasn't. We don't know.

At initial glance it seems to tell a straightforward story of the events that led to the Norman Conquest, and the Battle itself. But there is so much we do not understand: why the little figures in the upper and lower borders? Who were the few people named – Turold, the dwarf, and the woman, Alfgyva? Annoyingly, the makers did not include explanatory footnotes.

The Tapestry is a beautiful thing, even today its colours are bright and vibrant. It has survived wars and fires, and the skill that went into making it is as wondrous to us now, as it must have been back then, at some time soon after October 1066. The women who stitched it – for there was more than one hand responsible for its creation – put more than just thread into those scenes. There is sadness, loyalty, and love stitched there. But who designed it? Whose was the mind behind the Tapestry's creation?

'Naked!' I wriggled with a mixture of horror and delight as I stared up at my grandmother, my arms clutched around my knees. 'Tell me again, *Gammer*.'

My grandmother laughed. In the flickering firelight she looked like a young girl as she sat and stitched. 'I've told you the story a thousand times, little Elf.'

'Tell me again,' I begged. I hated to miss any part of the story.

'As a Saxon noblewoman it was my right to choose whom I would marry,' she began, as she always did. 'That will be your right too, Edith.'

My own marriage seemed very far away. 'You chose grandfather.' Some children called their grandfather *Gaffer*, but I did not. The Earl of Mercia, my grandfather, was kind, but stern. He scared me. He was often away, sometimes at the court of Wessex, or as far as Wales, so I did not know him as I knew my grandmother. With my own mother gone, I spent many weeks with Gammer in Coventry, in her beautiful hall, visiting the people in the town and farms, going to the monasteries and churches she endowed. And always, we rode. On horses so fine they seemed almost to fly across the plains, we spent hours on horseback, galloping all over my grandmother's lands, often as far as the wildwoods of Arden.

'Yes, I chose Leofric,' my grandmother said. The firelight caught the glimmer of her needle as she sewed, her stitches becoming faster. 'I didn't want to, at first. But many Saxon women have done what I was called to do. You know the name such women are given, those who marry to end war, or to bring lands and loyalties together. They are the *fripwebba*. Peace weavers.'

'Peace weavers.' I repeated the word slowly. I'd heard of them, of course. Many a night we sat at high table in Coventry hall, listening to the gleeman. My grandmother liked to hear the tale of *Beowulf* and Queen Wealtheow, the first *fripwebba*.

My grandmother chuckled. 'My marriage to Leofric was anything but peaceful.'

'Because of the ride.'

'Among other things. But who would want to marry a tame man?'

'Why did he make you ride … naked?' This time my voice hushed on the word, even though I knew the answer.

She was quiet for a moment, deep in thought, though she didn't drop a stitch. 'Because of the taxes. Leofric raised the *heregild* tax on the town of Coventry, to make up for funds Mercia had lost during the wars with the Danes. I knew these taxes would break my people, already threatened by famine. But Leofric would not listen. I begged him not impose the tax and to repeal the law. He refused. I persisted. I begged. Finally I declared that if he would revoke the tax I would ride in my shift as a penitent through the streets of Coventry.'

'Wearing only your shift!' I fingered the fine linen of my own shift beneath my tunic. It was thin, delicate. I would not like to ride in it. I preferred my leather leggings.

'I never dreamt he would take me at my word, or that he would dare me to do worse. He commanded me to ride –'

'Naked!' I broke in.

Gammer laughed. 'Now it was my turn to be daring. I

refused to give in. Your grandfather underestimated me. I said yes to his terrible challenge. I vowed to do it. It would be no shame to me, I declared, to bring justice to the people of Coventry.'

I gripped my fingers together, tight as a weave. 'Go on.'

My grandmother cast aside her sewing. 'The day of the ride arrived. My clothing was removed and I was naked upon my horse, with only my long hair to cover me.'

I touched my own braids. They were dark, and thick, but they wouldn't cover my body.

'The bells struck and I began to ride.' My grandmother's face took on a faraway look, as if she were on horseback once more. 'I forced myself to ride through the gates of the hall with my eyes half shut. When I opened them, to my astonishment, the main street wasn't crowded as I'd expected. Instead, it was eerily empty. No voices were heard, jeering or laughing. Instead, all I saw and heard as I approached were doors and shutters closing, as house by house, the people of Coventry turned their eyes away.'

'In gratitude, they would not look upon the nakedness of their beloved Lady Godiva,' I finished the tale as the townsfolk told it. 'All except for Peeping Tom. He looked out his window.'

My grandmother smiled. A sad, almost sorrowful smile. 'That's the tale.'

Sometimes I sensed there was much more to the story, something she wasn't telling me. But she wouldn't say any more as she picked up her embroidery.

'Enough weaving of tales, little Elf. It's time for your sewing lesson.'

Fripwebba. Peaceweaver.

To become a peaceweaver like my grandmother I laid the garland of sacred wedding herbs and flowers on my hair to wed Gruffydd ap Llewelyn of Wales. He was as grey-haired as my father, who I'd watched grow old after he'd inherited the Earldom of Mercia, only to lose it to Godwin, the Earl of Wessex.

My marriage brought my father a powerful ally. It also made me a Queen, but it did not make me a woman in love.

I'd hoped it would be for me as it had been for my grandmother, that I would fall in love with my husband, as she had. That I would care for him so much that I would forgive him anything, even having me ride naked through the town.

But I never grew to love Gruffydd. I loved our child, the only one who survived, a daughter we called Nest. I loved her with all the fierceness a mother can. But the love a woman has for a man, the love of tales and stories told at night by the gleeman, or over needle and thread around the fire, that I came to believe was mere myth.

I was wrong.

Harold Godwinson.

I knew his name. My father had cursed it, often enough.

An Earl, like my father. The second son of Godwin of Wessex, my father's sworn enemy. My father fought them to regain his own earldom. With my husband Gruffydd beside him they marched into England, sacking towns along the way. Winning, losing, winning, in a fight that seemed it would never end, until finally a peace treaty was arranged.

I wore moonstones the night I met Harold Godwinson, in a hall on the border of England and Wales where the treaty was signed.

Milky white, they crowned my head, laced my neck, clasped my sleeves. A silver trimmed tunic. I knew the stones suited my dark hair and pale skin. I wasn't beautiful, my heavy eyebrows were too fierce for that.

He was tall. Handsome. Strong.

Golden.

At high table he charmed all with his eloquence and ready jests. Almost all. He did not charm my father.

He barely glanced my way that night. I felt like a moth among the butterfly beauty of the court women with him. Gytha, his mother. Shrewd and still lovely. I sensed she would have enjoyed the company of my grandmother. Harold's sister Edythe. Outspoken and domineering, yet straightforward in her manner.

And another woman, impossible to overlook, who had no need for moonstones, or a domineering manner. The one they called Swan Neck, for her grace, or Richenda, for her beauty rich and fair. As golden as he. Glowing. Like something from a ballad, a tale.

Harold's wife. Edith. Her true name the same as mine.

The next day he sought me out in the herb garden. The sun lit his hair to brazen threads.

We stood apart, the air between us like a pulling tide.

'You're married,' he said.

'So are you,' I said.

He leaned in. His breath branded a tender place beneath my ear. 'You will not be married forever.'

When I became a widow, I waited. I waited to miss my husband, Gruffydd, who had died in peace, but to my shame I missed him not.

Instead, I sat by the window and stitched my embroidery, watching the castle gates.

When my grandmother visited, she stared. 'Edith. You are transformed.'

Morning, evening, first, last. Each thought, each stitch, binding him back to me.

I did not dare believe he would come for me.

Yet still I waited.

He came.

Harold took me in his arms. 'Now we are both free.'

'What of the other Edith?' I gasped when I came up for air, when his lips had searched mine as fiercely as my own. 'What of your wife?'

Her golden beauty had ghosted me. Thinking of her, melted with him.

He shrugged. 'Our marriage was a handfast. It can be set aside.'

Startled, I stepped back from him. 'You would break your oath?'

'Oaths are made to be broken. Any man who would be King knows that.'

'Is that what you want?' I asked. 'To be King?'

'I want to marry you.' He pulled me close. 'I vowed it when I saw you. We will have a Christian wedding.'

Such a wedding would be recognized in the eyes of the clergy, in the eyes of God. Many of the clergy, I knew, did not believe Harold and the other Edith's marriage to be a valid, Christian one. 'Surely she will protest.'

His jaw set. 'She will not complain. She has turned holy woman.'

Beautiful. Rich. Now holy, too.

His kiss pushed away my uneasiness at the way he seemed to cast her off without a care.

Harold and I married at Yuletide.

Some thought it a marriage of convenience, or political gain. That I was a peace weaver again, bringing Wales, Mercia and England together through my marriage.

Fate had woven a different thread into my wedding gown.

I wed the man I loved.

On our wedding night I released my hair. It floated over my naked body in black tendrils. It was long enough to cover me now. Through its web glinted the moonstones I wore on my naked skin.

He wrapped a strand around his finger. 'Edith. My wife.'

He'd said that before, to another woman. 'You have too many Ediths,' I retorted, to disguise the beating of my heart as he slid his fingers to silver parts of me that Gruffydd had never touched. 'Your sister. And the wife we now call your mistress. I refuse to be one among many.'

That other Edith had remained at court, disconcerting me whenever I met her blue gaze. Calm, watchful. Her head held high on her long neck. She made no complaints that her alliance – for I now refused to call it a marriage – was over. Their fair-haired children would still be recognized as Harold's.

His fingers explored deeper. 'You could never be one among many. But you're right. There are too many Ediths. Do you have no other name?'

'There is one,' I managed to reply, as waves of pleasure overcame me. 'A pet name my grandmother called me, as a child.'

'What is it?'

'As you know, my father was Elfgar. So my grandmother called me little Elf.'

'Elf.' His laugh became husky as his hands roamed. "A spirit. A nymph. But you feel real.'

"So do you." My hands were now on him. Learning the secrets of his golden-haired body.

With strands of my hair, I bound my husband to me, tighter than any handfast.

· · ·

Soon I was a Queen again, as well as a wife. In January 1066, at the behest of the *Witan* council, Harold was crowned King of England.

Anger at the news came fast from Normandy, where Duke William declared his greater right to the English throne. He'd begun to build warships, it was reported, seven hundred of them, ready to invade and claim what was his.

'Let the pretender come.' Harold raged. 'I'll beat him back from England's shores.'

Duke William also claimed that Harold had sworn fealty to him in Bayeux, when they were both in Normandy, and that Harold had vowed to uphold William's claim.

I twined my fingers together. 'It's said you swore on holy relics. Is it true?'

Harold cursed. 'I was William's hostage. I had to escape.'

He hadn't answered my question.

I remembered how easily he had set aside the other Edith.

'Oaths are made to be broken,' he'd told me. 'Any man who would be King knows that.'

Now, he was King.

A *ghost* of wind. A breath of air.

That's what changed our course. Or rather, William's course, for his ships were stranded for months, unable to attack England's shores.

Some said it was the work of vengeful spirits, some said it was the hand of God.

Harold waited for William on a coastal isle, ready to repel the Norman forces.

But the *ghost* lingered too long.

Harold ran out of provisions and abandoned his defence.

The wind changed. The Normans attacked.

Our lives unravelled.

'No!' I sobbed as I clung to him. 'I won't leave you!'

'Elf.' He stroked my face as the tears streamed down.

'Let me stay with you. Let me fight beside you. I can't leave you. I won't.'

'You're with child,' he said gently. 'You must be protected. How can I fight this battle if you are not safe?'

Still my tears flowed. I sobbed, shrieked, I who was usually so strong. It was as if all restraint had left me. All that was left was fear.

'No. No.'

He held me by the forearms. His eyes, fierce with love. 'Edith. My Elf. I beg you. Go to sanctuary with the other women of the court. Go *now*.'

He fell in battle. I knew it before I reached the safety of the convent walls. I knew it before we said good-bye. As if I had always known it. As if our every embrace had been farewell.

Later, two clerics came to the convent where we were clustered like fine-feathered hens.

We did not know them. One bowed to me. The other did not.

'Lady.' I noticed the one who spoke gave me no regal title. 'The Duke of Normandy has sent for your husband's body to be removed from the battlefield.'

No regal title for Harold, either.

'What's this?' His sister Edythe pushed forward. 'Are we allowed no burial for our King?'

'I offered the weight of my son's body in gold,' said Gytha, his mother. 'Name your price. More gold? I can pay it.'

'William wants no gold, and no shrine made for the King. And ...' The cleric who had bowed hesitated, glanced at me, and moved close to Edythe. He whispered in her ear.

She paled and crossed herself.

Pain knifed through me.

'What is it?' I clutched my belly in terror. 'Tell me!'

'They cannot identify the King's body.' Edythe's voice was a scrape, another twist of the knife. 'The arrow pierced his eye. After that, he was mutilated. He … he is in pieces.'

The room spun to blackness.

When I awoke, I was on the stone floor, the women around me.

I struggled to sit.

'Why have you come to tell women such news?' Edythe demanded, furious.

'The Duke wants the body identified.'

'Then have his knights do so.'

'It must be his wife.' The cleric who had refused to bow gave a sneer.

'There's only one part of him left intact.'

Again, the room spun, but this time I managed to remain sitting upright.

Edythe rushed at the cleric; her hand raised.

Gytha pulled her back, just in time.

The more courteous cleric coughed. 'There are marks only his wife would know.'

Holding down the bile I tried to stagger to my feet, only to collapse once more to the floor.

'You must not do it,' cried Harold's mother.

Edythe held me down as again I tried to rise. 'You cannot risk the babe!'

A quiet voice came from the corner. 'I will do it.'

She came to the centre of the room. Her beauty lit the dimness like a candle, even in the homespun linen gown she now favoured, with its band of Virgin blue around the hem.

'Not you!' Again, I struggled to stand, even as more pain sent my belly roiling. 'I am his wife. Not you!'

Her smile twisted with pity. 'Neither of us are wife now.'

At another pain in my belly, I buckled. It was as if my stomach had been pierced by an arrow too, so sharp was the pain. Yet I got to my feet, shaking off Edythe's hands.

'A stitch, nothing more.' I clutched my side. 'I will find him. Mend him. I must.'

'You cannot go in your state,' Gytha's voice shook. 'You carry Harold's child. I will not allow it.'

'It must be done,' said the cleric. 'And quickly.'

The other Edith came closer, sill quiet. 'I will take a priest.'

'I can accompany you,' the cleric said to her.

I took a step. Then another, that almost felled me. Finally, rasping for breath, I nodded.

It was hours before she returned.

When she came back the hem of her skirt was no longer blue.

Caked in mud. In bone. In blood. In gore.

Red.

He came to me in a dream. Empty sockets gushing with blood. I awoke with a stifled scream, clawing at my own face, my cheeks wet with tears.

Would the hideous visions never leave me? Surely the pain in my heart was a fatal wound that would soon take me from this world to be with him in the next. But the days dragged on, the sky as grey as the gown I wore. My eyes could not bear colour. Not green. Not yellow. Not red. The stone-grey walls of my nun's cell suited me. I rarely left it. I managed to eat, for the sake of the babe, but the food too was grey, its taste of ashes and stone.

It was in my cell my grandmother found me.

'Edith.'

I turned my face from the wall.

Gammer. What are you doing here?'

She frowned at my grey dress, my grey tone.

She drew up the wooden bench beside the bed where I lay. She wore no grey or black. The hem of her gown richly embroidered with flowers, day's eyes, rosemary and celandine, so finely sewn they must have been by her own hand. Glints of gold caught the gold that still threaded her hair, so bright that the rest shone silver.

'Why do you think I'm here? I sent word for you to come to me. I still have my lands in Coventry.'

'The Normans have left something then. The great conquerors.'

'Yes, I still have my home,' she said. 'But the Normans will have conquered indeed if my hall is no refuge for those I love.'

Tears welled in my eyes as she stroked my hand. 'Edith. Edith. You are losing the battle.'

'It's already been lost.' My voice was a raven's caw.

'No.' Her face was fierce now, beautiful. 'You must be brave. You are a Saxon, whose women do not give up. Have I not always taught you to keep the Saxon way? Don't you remember the tales I told you, the stories of heroes, men and women both, in days gone by? I told you those stories for a reason.'

'What good are stories? Old wives' tales.' I scoffed, even though I knew it would hurt her.

Instead, she smiled. 'Stories are what last in the end. Don't you understand that yet? They're as real as love or courage or honour or kindness. Though we can't see these things, they are all that matter.'

'All that matters is gone. Love. And courage. And honour. And kindness. I have nothing left.'

'You have something left.' She reached into a leather

pouch. From it she pulled a sharp glint of gold, brighter than her hair.

The point pierced my palm as she thrust it into my hand. 'The needle can mend. The sword cannot.'

The colours were so bright they hurt my eyes.

Blue.

Like the sky on the day we wed.

Yellow.

Like the *korn* fields of Coventry.

Like my grandmother's hair.

Green.

Like the leaves in the wildwoods of Arden, where I played as a child.

Grey.

Like the stones of the convent walls.

Red.

I shuddered as I folded out the linen, white as a shroud, and picked up the first length of wool.

I would start with red.

Battles. Ships. Knights. Shields. Horns. Birds. Fish. Beasts. Fields. A dragon-tailed star in the sky.

'I didn't want this,' my grandmother said, disapproving, when she came to the convent where I had stayed and found me hard at work, eyes strained, fingers sore.

In the basket beside me skeins of wool had become tangled. I pulled on a thread and refilled the needle.

Harold's mother Gytha came to visit me. I was at my work.

'You are making a gift for the Conqueror?'

Biting off a thread I nodded.

She stared at me as if I had lost my wits.

'Why?'

'The truth must be told.'

'The Normans do not want our truth. They want our tales to be lost. That's how they conquer. By taking our lands, our language, our songs and stories.'

'They will not know it is my work. My thread will twist the tale. What is revealed is what is concealed.'

She tossed her head, impatiently. 'You speak in riddles.'

'I tell the story two ways. By hand, by stitch. This embroidery will seem as if it praises William. Yet it is Harold my work will praise.'

'Show me.'

Carefully I unrolled the linen.

'Here is the tale I tell of Harold. I have started it from before the battle, from when he went to Normandy, to Bayeux, and met William.'

Gytha exhaled. 'When he was first betrayed by the Norman Duke and his lies.'

I showed her the depiction of Harold at prayer. 'See here,' I said. 'Here he prays, devout. It is a good picture of him, as a Godly man. But below, here,' I pointed to the birds that grovelled on the ground, 'Here is William. The ungodly.'

She peered closer, smiled, and then frowned.

'Surely the Normans will be able to tell you mock the Conqueror?'

I shook my head. 'I think not. Those who are so proud cannot see themselves in a poor light. They can only judge others by it.'

Sewing was the way to do it, I'd decided, for stitches must hold true. The story must not be told from the Saxon side alone, or it would be destroyed. I would make it so artful that no one could bear to destroy it. I would not flatter Harold nor William, but tell the truth as it was. Two-sided.

'Show me some more,' Gytha demanded, imperious.

'Here is our King,' for that was the title I still gave him, in such company.

'Here he is at feast. And here are the Norman wolves that surround him, licking their paws.'

'But they will read it as if it is Harold who is crafty.'

'In the language of fable, yes.' I nodded. 'Even the Normans know Æsop's tales.'

I laughed at the thought of the work perhaps being hung in a Norman court. There would be secret jibes against those in whose very halls it hung, for those who had eyes to see it.

My laugh was as rusty as an old needle.

'I think my Lord would have liked this one. Here he rides high,' I indicated him mounted, noble on a horse, 'and here he makes love like a lecher.'

If I thought to shock Gytha, just as I could never shock my grandmother, I could not. She gave a bawdy chuckle. 'Like father like son.'

It was I who blushed. To hide my embarrassment, I pointed to the crow poised in a tree.

'Here is the fabled crow,' I said. 'Who taunts and boasts of his own prowess. It may be thought to be Harold who boasts and was then defeated. But this embroidery is my fable. Here I tell the tale. It is William who crows, yet secretly I defeat him. My sword is my needle.'

She stared at it in wonder, unfolded more. When she raised her eyes, they were alight, no longer dulled with a grief as grey as mine.

'Edith.' Gytha begged me now. 'You must let me help. It is too much work for one pair of hands. The whole story must be recounted. I can put women to work, many skilled with the needle.'

'None must know our true purpose,' I warned.

'My women will do as they are told.'

I was sure they would.

In the end, it was not only Gytha's women who sewed.

Word spread by stealth, whispered among women, in halls, houses and cloisters across England. Pieces were described in code, stitched in secret. Other scenes were sewed openly. Harold's sister Edythe snorted. 'Men never take notice of what women are doing.'

Some women, widows, mothers of lost sons, gave pieces of wool. Some sent needles, sharp as knives. My own beloved daughter, Nest, made for her part a red dragon, the creature of Wales. Harold's sister Edythe worked with skill and speed, often by my side at the convent. She joined together the pieces as it grew, like a banner unfurled.

And my grandmother, of course, she sewed too. Horses, mostly. And lions. For Leofric, her husband, the lionhearted. My grandmother's ancient nurse, now blind, sewed day and night, for the darkness did not bother her. She needed no candle.

Sometimes I too sewed by the light of the moon and no other. Sometimes it seemed I sewed by night and by day, for now my night dreams were full of stitches.

One morning, when I awoke, I thought to be in a dream, for a vision of golden beauty stood before me. Wrapped even as she was in a thick, travel stained cloak, the loveliness of her face and figure could not be disguised.

We sewed all day, in silence. She was not as skilled at the art as I, but her stiches were even and fine, her long neck bent to the task.

'Thank you,' she said, when the work was done.

I looked at the picture she had made after she had gone. It was a house on fire with a woman and child fleeing from it.

I never saw her again. But I heard, later, from my grandmother, that she had fled a house burned by the Normans. Her sewing was a message of survival, or triumph, perhaps.

'She was braver than me,' I said, ashamed.

'There are many forms of courage,' my grandmother said gently.

I would need it for when the babe was born, our child who would never see his father.

Faster and faster I sewed.

I wove myself into the tale.

One night my grandmother halted my hand, laid hers over my restless fingers. 'You cannot sew much more, Edith.'

'I've almost finished my part,' I said.

She looked at my design curiously. 'I can't make out the meaning of this section. It's a puzzle.'

I pointed to the veiled, fine dressed woman I'd embroidered. She stood out, for apart from the scene of the burning house the other Edith had made, there was only one other scene depicting a woman.

'You can see this is a Saxon noblewoman,' I said to my grandmother.

My grandmother nodded. 'Of course. By her veil, her tunic.'

I pointed to the tonsured man who touched the noblewoman's face. 'To some she will appear to be struck across the face by this cleric, struck by the hand of God for her sins. To others, she will appear to be receiving holy instruction, being chosen for a sacred task.'

'The tapestry.'

'Yes.'

That night my pains began.

I stitched on and on until I could almost do no more.

Yet it wasn't complete. Not yet.

Waters broke around me. I gritted my teeth and worked on. I sewed the man's naked body. Whole. Intact. Set him below the woman and God's hand.

At last, it was finished.

Above my final scene I signed my work, between two red dragons.

One word.

Each letter a strain, a push.

At last, it was complete. The black thread broken.

Ælfgyva.

Elf's Gift.

The needle slipped from my hand.

AUTHOR'S NOTE

For centuries, there has been dispute over the origins of the Bayeux Tapestry. Did Flemish, French women make it? Did English women? Does it praise William the Conqueror or subtly mock him? Or is it King Harold who is mocked? And who is the 'Mysterious Lady' featured on the tapestry, with the name 'Aelfgyva'?

In this tale, I knew I wanted it to include my personal heroine, Lady Godiva, the subject of *Naked: A Novel of Lady Godiva*. As she was the grandmother (or step-grandmother) to Edith, wife of Harold, it was easy to imagine she passed on some traits and skills to her granddaughter. I wanted to capture the power of women in the tales they weave, and no more is this revealed than in the mysterious fabric of the Bayeux Tapestry. It is a work of art, secret and legend that has stood the test of time.

In Lady Godiva's lifetime, a popular Saxon saying was 'Men wield weapons while women weave'. (In *Naked*, Godiva also wields a sword, but that's another story.) Yet the needle, like the pen, has its own power. Before 1066 the word 'mend' had two meanings. One was to repair, the other was to make right or remove a fault, to make 'amends'. In the end, the needle may indeed be mightier than the sword.

Eliza Redgold
www.elizaredgold.com

DISCUSSION SUGGESTIONS

What is the difference between embroidery and tapestry?
Can you think of any other such commemorative items that
survive to tell the tales of the past?

Have you any thoughts on what the little images (some of
them sexually explicit) along the borders of the Bayeux
Tapestry could mean?

ENDWORD
HELEN HOLLICK

From the germ of an idea an entire book has blossomed and grown. Enriched by enthusiasm, passion – and hard work – the result, we hope, will prove to be rewarding. The eclectic mix of stories have given us, a diverse group of writers, great pleasure to produce. Although a joint effort, we were all responsible for our own contributions, from the initial idea, through the writing, rewriting and editing process, to the final proofreading. On behalf of us all, thank you to our various editors who, hopefully picked up any bloopers.

Also to Cathy Helms of www.avalongraphics.org for the wonderful award-winning cover design, and the delightful C.C. Humphreys for his inspiring foreword.

This second edition, published by my own Taw River Press, has been just as much hard – but enjoyable – work to produce. The original edition was e-book only, I am so pleased that we now also have an edition available in paperback.

Historical fiction is occasionally a Cinderella genre, often eschewed by some academics who claim it is not 'proper' history, and discussed in depth, even by its stalwart supporters – should novels about history be as accurate with the 'facts' as possible? Does historical romance, complete with semi-naked hunks and women with heaving bosoms, count as historical fiction? Then there is historical mystery, thrillers, adventure, fantasy, steampunk – basically anything set in the past (usually at least fifty years ago) now counts as historical fiction. And despite what some bookstores may claim, the genre, with *all* its sub-genres, is immensely popular.

But what of *alternative* history, where what actually happened is altered in some small or great way? No, it is not 'factual' history, it is *imaginative* fiction, written perhaps tongue-in-cheek or to explore 'what if?' possibilities – as we do here in *1066 Turned Upside Down*.

In my personal view, the whole point of fiction – *any* fiction – is to create cracking good stories that are a cracking good read. Authors have a 'duty of care' to get the known facts right – otherwise the entire believability of a story could be ruined – but does it matter if the story is true or not? I hope, in this particular case, no, it doesn't!

Helen Hollick
2021

ABOUT THE AUTHORS

Alison Morton

Alison Morton writes the award-winning Roma Nova thriller series featuring tough, but compassionate heroines. She blends her deep love of Roman history with six years' military service and a life of reading crime, historical, adventure and thriller fiction. On the way, she collected a BA in modern languages and an MA in history.

All six full-length Roma Nova novels have won the BRAG Medallion, the prestigious award for indie fiction. Two novellas and a collection of short stories complete the series (so far!). *Successio*, *Aurelia* and *Insurrectio* were selected as Historical Novel Society's Indie Editor's Choices. *Aurelia* was a finalist in the 2016 HNS Indie Award. *The Bookseller* selected *Successio* as Editor's Choice in its inaugural indie review.

A 'Roman nut' since age 11, Alison misspent decades clambering over Roman sites throughout Europe. Fascinated by the mosaics at Ampurias (Spain), at their creation by the complex, power and value-driven Roman civilisation, she started wondering what a modern Roman society would be like if run by strong women.

And what else could have happened in history in such an alternative timeline…

Now she continues to write thrillers and has recently branched out into a contemporary crime setting with *Double Identity*, the first of a planned series. In between writing Alison cultivates a Roman herb garden and drinks wine in France with her husband.

Website www.alison-morton.com

Anna Belfrage

Had Anna been allowed to choose, she'd have become a time-traveller. As this was impossible, she became a financial professional with two absorbing interests: history and writing. Anna has authored the acclaimed time travelling series *The Graham Saga*, set in 17th century Scotland and Maryland, as well as the equally acclaimed medieval series *The King's Greatest Enemy* which is set in 14th century England.

Anna has also published *The Wanderer*, a fast-paced contemporary romantic suspense trilogy with paranormal and time-slip ingredients. Her September 2020 release, *His Castilian Hawk,* has her returning to medieval times. Set against the complications of Edward I's invasion of Wales, *His Castilian Hawk* is a story of loyalty, integrity—and love. Her most recent release, *The Whirlpools of Time*, is a time travel romance set against the backdrop of brewing rebellion in the Scottish highlands.

All of Anna's books have been awarded the IndieBRAG Medallion, she has several Historical Novel Society Editor's Choices, and one of her books won the HNS Indie Award in 2015. Her books have been reviewed by Discovering Diamonds – several having been shortlisted for Book of the Month and Cover of the Month. She is also the proud recipient of various Reader's Favourite medals as well as having won various Gold, Silver and Bronze Coffee Pot Book Club awards.

Find out more about Anna, her books and her eclectic historical blog on her website www.annabelfrage.com

Annie Whitehead

Annie is an historian and prize-winning author. Her main interest in history is the rich seam of stories to be found in the period formerly known as the 'Dark Ages' and she strives to bring these people into the spotlight to portray them more as medieval characters than mythical folk who dwell among dragons and elves.

Her first novel, *To Be A Queen*, is the story of Aethelflaed (daughter of Alfred the Great), who came to be known as the Lady of the Mercians. It was long-listed for the Historical Novel Society's Indie Award 2016 and was an IAN finalist in 2017. *Alvar the Kingmaker*, tells the story of Aelfhere of Mercia, a nobleman in the time of King Edgar, who sacrifices personal happiness in order to keep the monarchy strong when successive kings die at a young age. Her third novel, *Cometh the Hour* goes further back in time to the seventh century, to tell the story of Penda, the last pagan king of Mercia. All of her novels have won IndieBRAG medallions.

Annie has twice been a prizewinner in the *Mail on Sunday* Novel Writing competition, she won first prize for nonfiction in the new *Writing Magazine* Poetry and Prose competition, and she has had articles published in various magazines, on a wide range of topics. She was the inaugural winner of the HWA (Historical Writers' Association)/Dorothy Dunnett Society Short Story Competition and is now a judge for that same competition.

Annie has had two nonfiction books published. *Mercia: The Rise and Fall of a Kingdom* (Amberley Books) has been an Amazon #1 Bestseller. *Women of Power in Anglo-Saxon England* was published by Pen & Sword Books in 2020.

Also in 2020, she was a contributor to the anthology of historical stories, *Betrayal*. The Historical Novel Society review said of her story that it 'provides a sweeping scope, fine period details, and beautiful writing.'

Website www.anniewhiteheadauthor.co.uk

Carol McGrath

Following her first degree in Russian Studies, English and History, Carol McGrath completed an MA in Creative Writing at The Seamus Heaney Centre, Belfast, followed by an MPhil from University of London. She is the author of *The Daughters of Hastings Trilogy*. Her fifth historical novel, *The Silken Rose*, first in The Rose Trilogy, published by the Headline Group, is set during the High Middle Ages. It features Ailenor of Provence and was published in 2020. *The Damask Rose* about Eleanor of Castile was published in 2021. *The Stone Rose*, Isabella of France, follows in 2022.

Carol has also written Historical Non-Fiction for Pen & Sword.

Website www.carolcmcgrath.co.uk

C.C. Humphreys

Chris (C.C.) Humphreys has played Hamlet in Calgary, a gladiator in Tunisia, waltzed in London's West End, conned the landlord of the Rovers Return in *Coronation Street*, Walked the Sun Hill beat in *The Bill*, commanded a starfleet in *Andromeda*, voiced Salem the cat in the original *Sabrina*, and is a dead immortal in *Highlander*.

Chris has written several historical fiction novels including:

The French Executioner, runner-up the CWA Steel Dagger for Thrillers; *Chasing the Wind*; *The Jack Absolute Trilogy*; *Vlad - The Last Confession*; *A Place Called Armageddon* and *Shakespeare's Rebel* which he adapted into a play and which premiered at Bard on the Beach, Vancouver, in 2015.

Plague won the Arthur Ellis Award for Best Crime Novel in Canada in 2015.

Chris has an MFA in Creative Writing from the University of British Columbia. He is now writing epic fantasy with the *Immortals' Blood Trilogy*, for Gollancz. The first two books, *Smoke in the Glass* and *The Coming of the Dark* are now published. The epic finale, *The Wars of Gods and Men* will be out in 2022.

Several of his novels are available as Audiobooks - read by himself! He has a new novel just out: *One London Day* - a modern London Noir. Quite a different adventure.

Chris lives in a forest overlooking a fjord on Salt Spring Island, BC, Canada.

Website www.authorchrishumphreys.com

Eliza Redgold

Eliza Redgold is an author and 'romantic academic'. Her natural pen name is based upon the old, Gaelic meaning of her name, Dr Elizabeth Reid Boyd. English folklore has it that if you help a fairy, you will be rewarded with red gold.

Her bestselling historical fiction includes her *Ladies of Legend* trilogy, starting with *Naked: A Novel of Lady Godiva* released internationally by St Martin's Press, New York. Her historical romances are published by Harlequin Historical, London (Harper Collins). They include *Playing the Duke's Mistress*, *Enticing Benedict Cole*, *The Scandalous Suffragette* and *The Master's New Governess*. They have been translated into multiple languages including Italian, Polish, Czech, Danish and Swedish, and are available internationally.

Website www.elizaredgold.com

G.K. Holloway

After graduating from Coventry University with an honours degree in history and politics, he worked in education in and around Bristol, England, where he now lives.

After reading a biography about Harold Godwinson, he

studied the late Anglo-Saxon era in detail and visited all of the locations mentioned in the sources. When he had enough material to weave together facts and fiction he produced his novel. *1066 What Fates Impose* is the product of all that research – along with some additional imagination.

1066 What Fates Impose is a story of family feuds, court intrigues, assassinations, plotting and scheming, loyalty and love, all ingredients in an epic struggle for the English crown.

Website www.gkholloway.co.uk

Helen Hollick

Helen moved from London in 2013 and now lives on a thirteen-acre farm in North Devon, England, with her husband, daughter, son-in-law, and a variety of animals.

Born in London, Helen wrote pony stories as a teenager, moved to science fiction and fantasy, and then discovered the wonder of historical fiction. Published since 1994 with her Arthurian *Pendragon's Banner Trilogy*, which was followed by her 1066 era duo. She became a *USA Today* bestseller with her story of Queen Emma: *The Forever Queen* (titled *A Hollow Crown* in the UK), and its companion novel, *Harold the King* (titled *I Am the Chosen King* in the U.S.A).

She also writes the *Sea Witch Voyages*, a series of pirate-based nautical adventures with a touch of fantasy.

Commissioned by Amberley Press she wrote a non-fiction book about pirates in fact, fantasy and fiction, published in 2017, and also a non-fiction book about smugglers, published by Pen and Sword.

Recently she has ventured into the 'Cosy Mystery' genre with her Jan Christopher Mysteries, the first of which is *A Mirror Murder*.

She has achieved IndieBRAG medallions, and Chill With A Book awards, and has been a guest on Radio Devon on several occasions.

She blogs regularly, and after leaving the Historical Novel Society as Managing Editor for Indie Reviews in 2016, has organised *Discovering Diamonds*, an independent online review site for Historical Fiction, primarily aimed at showcasing Indie writers.

She occasionally gets time to write.

Website www.helenhollick.net

Joanna Courtney

Ever since Joanna sat up in her cot with a book, she'd wanted to be a writer and she wrote endless stories, plays and Enid-Blyton-style novels as a child. Her favourite subjects at school were English and history, and at Cambridge University she combined these passions by studying medieval literature. Nowadays she pours them into writing historical fiction.

Joanna cut her publication teeth on short stories and serials for the women's magazines before signing to PanMacmillan in 2014 for her three-book series *The Queens of the Conquest* about the wives of the men fighting to be King of England in 1066. It is an endless frustration to her that the stories of this great year are so relentlessly male, despite the undoubted power of the women fighting for the throne alongside their husbands, and she set out to release their stories.

Her second series, written for Piatkus, takes the same aim of liberating women from the bonds of history but this time less from obscurity than from misrepresentation. *Shakespeare's Queens* explores the real history of three of the bard's greatest female characters – Lady Macbeth, much-loved ruler of Scotland for some fifteen years from 1025; Ophelia, shield-maiden and right-hand warrior to Prince Hamlet in 600 BC; and Cordelia, one of three honoured princesses in the matriarchy of the Coritani tribe back in 500 BC.

Joanna's fascination with historical writing is in finding the similarities between us and them – the core humanness of people throughout the ages – with an especial goal to provide a female take on some of the greatest stories we think we know...

Website www.joannacourtney.com

Richard Dee

Richard Dee was a Master Mariner and ship's pilot, now living in Brixham, South Devon. Years spent travelling the real world in the Merchant Navy inspired him to create new places and times for his characters to explore. Before retirement his working life saw him flirting with various jobs, including Dockmaster, Marine Insurance Surveyor and Port Control Officer, finally becoming a Thames Pilot. He regularly took vessels of all sizes through the Thames Barrier and upriver as far as London Bridge.

His novels include Science Fiction and Steampunk adventures, *The Rocks of Aserol*, *Freefall* and *Ribbonworld* among others, as well as the exploits of Andorra Pett, a reluctant amateur detective. You can find out about his life and writing on his website www.richarddeescifi.co.uk

BEFORE YOU GO

Finally, if you have enjoyed any or all of our 'what if' stories, please do leave us a comment on Amazon and Goodreads.

Thank you.

Lightning Source UK Ltd.
Milton Keynes UK
UKHW012216130223
416920UK00006B/1036